THIS TIME WON'T YOU SAVE ME

KYIRIS ASHLEY

URBAN AINT DEAD

URBAN AINT DEAD
P.O Box 448
Maybrook, NY 12543

Cover Design: P. Wise / The Wise Services

Edited By: Shawna Brim / Ladies of Lit

Contact Author on FB: Kyiris Ashley / IG: @kyirisashley

Contact Publisher at www.urbanaintdead.com

Email: urbanaintdead@gmail.com

ISBN: 979-8-9902387-7-0

CONTENTS

SOUNDTRACKS

Scan the QR Code below to listen to the Soundtracks/Singles
of some of your favorite U.A.D titles:

Don't have Spotify or Apple Music?
No Sweat!
Visit your choice streaming platform and search URBAN
AINT DEAD.

URBAN AINT DEAD

Like & Follow us on social media:
FB - URBAN AINT DEAD
IG: @urbanaintdead
Tik Tok - @urbanaintdead

SUBMISSIONS

Submit the first three chapters of your completed manuscript to urbanaintdead@gmail.com, subject line: Your book's title. The manuscript must be in a .doc file and sent as an attachment. The document should be in Times New Roman, double-spaced, and in size 12 font. Also, provide your synopsis and full contact information. If sending multiple submissions, they must each be in a separate email. Have a story but no way to submit it electronically? You can still submit to URBAN AINT DEAD. Send in the first three chapters, written or typed, of your completed manuscript to:

URBAN AINT DEAD
P.O Box 448
Maybrook, NY 12543

DO NOT send original manuscript. Must be a duplicate.
Provide your synopsis and a cover letter containing your full
contact information.
Thanks for considering URBAN AINT DEAD.

CHAPTER ONE

"Happy birthday to you! Happy birthday, dear Aspen, happy birthday to you!" The crowd sang as Aspen looked around at their smiling faces. It was her tenth birthday, and the entire neighborhood had come out to help her celebrate. Her parents had thrown her the biggest princess party any of them had ever seen. Their entire backyard was decorated with every princess Disney ever made. There were hundreds of balloons everywhere with flower sculptures of the princesses. Her father was on the grill, cooking up slabs of ribs and pounds of chicken thighs and wings, while the DJ was on the table spinning the ones and twos. Aspen's parents had even hired a bartender to tend their backyard bar. She mixed cocktails for the adults and snow cones for all the children. The entire party was a vibe, and everyone was enjoying themselves. They all stood around the cake table as they waited for Aspen to blow out the candles on the top of her three-tier cake.

"Make a wish, baby girl," Shantelle requested.

Shantelle was Aspen's mother. She was a beautiful caramel complected woman with shoulder length hair that she kept in a blunt cut. The color of her hair depended on the season and, at the moment, it was blonde. She stood five feet two inches tall and had a shape that most women would pay for. Her beautiful gray eyes gave her an exotic look, and she'd passed those same gray eyes down to her daughters.

Aspen closed her eyes, making a wish, before blowing out her candles. The crowd clapped and cheered, and Shantelle began removing the candles from the cake. Shantelle cut the cake, handing the first piece to Aspen before handing plates to the rest of the partygoers.

"I can't believe my baby girl is ten years old already. Where did the time go?" Shantelle spoke, wrapping her arms around Aspen, hugging her tightly.

"Ma, I can't breathe. You squeezing me too tight," Aspen blurted, trying to release herself from her mother's grasp.

"I need to keep you close. You growing up on me too fast," Shantelle joked, kissing Aspen's forehead.

"Aww, Mom, come on now. My friends are here. Don't kiss me. I'm ten years old now. Ain't it a cut off limit for kissin' me in public?" Aspen asked.

"Girl, shut up. Cove is fifteen, and I still kiss her goodbye every time she leaves," Shantelle informed, referring to her oldest daughter. She kissed Aspen again before running her hands over Aspen's long, brown pigtails.

Shantelle and her husband had been together since their freshmen year of high school. Shantelle became pregnant at just fifteen years old with their oldest daughter, Cove. Everyone around her told Shantelle the relationship wouldn't last. Her mother had even taken her to get an abortion, telling Shantelle she was too young to have a baby. However, at the last minute, Shantelle jumped up from the table and ran out the clinic.

"If you keep that boy's baby, you gonna get the fuck outta my house. I'm not takin' care of no more kids. You wanna be grown, then do that shit on yo own. You think that boy gonna help you raise that baby? Well, I'm here to tell you that he ain't. You gonna be a single mama just like the rest of us. Oh, and when he leaves yo ass, you can't come back here cause I told yo dumb ass not to have that baby in the first place," Shantelle's mother spat evilly as she looked at her daughter with disgust.

She knew boys like Mario only wanted one thing, and after they got it, they would leave, never to be heard from again. It was the same thing that happened to her and her mother as well. She knew it would be no different for her daughter, so she tried to save her from the same heartache she'd experienced.

"I don't need you to do nothing for me or my baby. You just bitter cause ain't no man ever loved you. You got two kids, and neither one of our daddies wanted you!" Shantelle yelled back, walking out of the house, never looking back again.

Shantelle and Mario had been married for the past eight years and now had two beautiful daughters together. They lived in a huge, five-bedroom home in the Boston Edison district of Detroit, Michigan. Ever since he was a teen, Mario had a dream of being the biggest drug dealer Detroit had ever seen. Now, years later, all his hard work had paid off, putting Mario and his brother, Donté, at the top of the food chain. Drug dealers from across all fifty states came to Detroit to buy their drugs from Mario and Donté. Not only did they have the best product in the United States, but they also had the best prices, making it easy for them to make millions from the drug business alone.

Mario stood six feet two inches tall with skin so smooth it resembled melted dark chocolate. He rocked a low-cut Caesar with deep waves and sideburns that faded into his clean-cut goatee. Every gold digger in the city wanted him, but he had never stepped out on Shantelle. She was the love of his life and the only woman he wanted.

"Aspen, I brought my swimsuit. Let's get in the pool," Brianna cheered. Brianna was Aspen's best friend, and she loved her like a sister. They'd met two years before on the first day of third grade. They'd been inseparable ever since.

"Okay, let me go put mine on," Aspen replied, running into the house and up to her room. She quickly changed into her swimsuit before going back outside, meeting up with Brianna, and jumping into the pool.

"Mama, do I have to stay for the whole party? I was trying to hit the mall with Jayla and Sade," Cove questioned, walking up to Shantelle.

Cove was the "it" girl —both in school and on the block. She was a beautiful young lady that looked just like her mother. Every young hustler wanted her but would never try due to the fear her father put in them. She had flowing brown hair that she kept in all the latest styles from the weekly salon appointments she attended with her mother and sister. Her chocolate skin was the only thing she'd inherited from her father while everything else, including those signature gray eyes, was given to her straight from her mother.

"Yes, girl, you gotta stay. How you think Aspen is going to feel if her only sister leaves her party?"

"She not even paying me no mind. She out there having fun with her friends. She don't even notice me, so if I leave, it would be the same thing," Cove countered. Before Shantelle could say another word, Mario came over to them.

"How are two of my three favorite girls doing?"

"Daddy, Mama won't let me go to the mall with Jayla and Sade. Talking 'bout I can't leave Aspen's party. It's only three more Saturdays left before we go back to school. I don't want to spend them at home. Why can't I go with my friends?" Cove whined.

Cove knew that by asking her daddy, she would get whatever she was asking for. Mario Billups had never been the type of parent to tell his children no. Growing up poor as a child, his main goal was to provide his children with the life he'd never had. It didn't matter how much something cost or how much time had to go into it. If it was something his daughters wanted, then he was going to make it happen. Reaching into his wallet, Mario pulled out several blue bills and handed them to Cove.

"Go have fun." Mario spoke.

"Mario, she needs…"

"Let it go, Shantelle. It's nothing but kids here. Let Cove go be a teenager," Mario demanded, cutting his wife off mid-sentence.

Mario pulled his wife closer to him, kissing her on the lips. Shantelle didn't protest anymore as she kissed her husband back passionately. "Okay, nah, don't start nothing you can't finish," Shantelle challenged.

Mario smiled, slapping his wife on her plump ass before heading back to the grill and watching Aspen as she played in the pool. A white Range Rover pulled up, and Mario saw the smile spread across Aspen's face. Her favorite uncle had just arrived.

"Uncle Donté, Uncle Donté," Aspen yelled, jumping out of the pool, and running over to her uncle, not even bothering to grab a towel and dry off first.

"What up doe, lil bit? Happy birthday," Donté greeted, smiling, showing all thirty-two of his pearly white teeth. He was tall and muscular, just as Mario was. In fact, they looked just alike, only Donté was light skinned with locs.

"Are those presents for me?" Aspen asked, pointing to the two huge gift bags in Donté's hands.

"You already know they are. You know I wasn't coming to yo party without gifts. Ten years old is a big deal," Donté informed, handing Aspen the gift bags.

"Thank you, Uncle Donté!" Aspen cooed, taking the bags, and running off with them.

"Look at you spoiling her even more. I swear ain't none of them lil snot nose niggas gonna be able to bare minimum my babies. Daddy and Unc been showing them real love since birth," Mario stated, walking up to greet Donté.

"And if they try, I trust my Glock to handle it," Donté announced, double tapping his hip.

"What up doe, bro? I'm glad you could make it." Mario spoke, slapping hands with his brother.

"Shit, you knew damn well I wasn't missin' lil bit's party for nothing in the world."

"Yeah, you right. I knew her favorite uncle was gonna be here if no one else was. Yo, after the party, I wanna talk to you about a few things."

"Fasho. I'm chillin'. I ain't going nowhere no time soon. I'm 'bout to get me a plate of some of dem good ass ribs, have me a few beers, and enjoy my niece's party."

"Cool, let me get back over to this grill and check this food."

. . .

THE PARTY STARTED WRAPPING up around eight that evening. All the neighborhood children had to be home once the streetlights came on, and that took away over half of the party. Once the rest of the children that went to her school went home, it was only Brianna and Aspen still inside the pool.

"You should spend the night. Let's call yo mama and ask her. Tell her we wanna play with all the new toys I got for my birthday," Aspen suggested.

"Okay, but you ask her. She not gonna tell you no," Brianna reasoned.

The two friends wrapped themselves in a towel, running off, heading up to Aspen's room.

"Ms. Shanté, please. It's my birthday, and Brianna is my best friend," Aspen begged.

"I'll tell you what. After we leave our family reunion tomorrow, I'll bring Brianna back over, and she can spend the night then. Deal?" Shanté suggested.

The girls looked over at each other, figuring they should take the deal. When they both agreed, Shanté told Brianna she would be picking her up within twenty minutes.

"Girl, you got so many gifts. You lucky to be rich," Brianna uttered, eyeing the dozens of gifts Aspen received.

"We not rich. Rich is the people on TV that live in huge mansions. This is just a house," Aspen responded.

"Yeah, a really big house." Brianna laughed.

．　．　．

"So, what's up, bro? What you wanted to talk about?" Donté asked, taking a seat across from Mario in his home office.

"What you think about the Chi-town niggas?"

"You talkin' 'bout Moe and Duke? They cool. We been doing a lot of business with them lately. They been coming, getting big ass shipments like every other week," Donté stated.

"Exactly. You don't see nothing wrong with that? They going through a lot of kilos. Shit just seems weird to me. I don't know 'bout them, bro."

"What you thinkin', they the police or some shit?" Donté asked.

"Nah, I don't think they the police. We would have been locked up if that was the case. But it's something not right with them niggas."

"I hear you, bro. We gonna keep an eye on them. From now on, we won't go meet them alone. When they come to re-up, we both go," Donté suggested.

The brothers continued to converse over a few drinks until Donté decided it was time to leave. Mario walked up to his bedroom, ready to relax for the night. When he walked inside the room, he saw candles lit all around. He smiled at the romantic setting his wife created. He walked inside their en suite bathroom and saw Shantelle standing there, pouring champagne into two flutes. She'd ran them a hot bath and had the tub filled with bubbles and rose petals.

"Aspen is asleep, and Cove is spending the night at her friend's house. It's our time now," Shantelle informed, handing Mario a glass.

"Oh, you ready, huh?" Mario questioned, taking a sip of champagne.

"Are you ready is the real question," Shantelle whispered, reaching down and unbuckling Mario's belt, pulling both his pants and boxers down to the floor. Smiling at what she saw, she allowed him to finish his champagne before she removed his shirt.

They both stepped into the water with Shantelle straddling Mario in their huge jacuzzi tub. Mario took her breast in his hands before flicking both nipples with his tongue. Shantelle threw her head back as she moaned in pleasure.

"I wanna feel that dick, baby," Shantelle whispered, taking her husband's manhood into her hands.

"Put it in then," he challenged.

Shantelle wasted no time easing her soft wetness down onto him, housing his width as his girth filled her. She moaned softly as she grinded on him in slow circles, forming her rhythm in her head as she listened to the waves she made with the water. She felt Mario grip her ass tightly with his hands, and she grinded harder.

"Damn, baby, ride that dick. Ride this dick like you love this muthafucka," Mario moaned as his eyes rolled in the back of his head in pure ecstasy.

"Yeah, bitch, ride that dick like you love it cause that's the last dick you ever gonna ride." A male voice spoke smugly, startling both Mario and Shantelle.

"W-what the fuck are y'all doing in my got damn house?" Mario yelled, looking up at all three of the masked men.

"Shut the fuck up, nigga. I'm the one asking the questions around this muthafucka." The man's deep voice spoke. Walking over to Mario, he hit him in the mouth with the butt of his gun.

"Ahhh," Shantelle screamed before covering her mouth with both her hands, afraid of being hit as well. It was then that she thought about her daughter, who was sleeping in her room down the hall. She didn't want to make too much noise and wake Aspen, knowing she would walk into their room and be faced with three masked men.

"Please, take whatever you want and just leave," Shantelle pleaded.

She was terrified, and all she wanted was for the men to leave. She saw three men in front of her but was unaware if there was anyone else inside their home. *Oh, my God, what if there's someone already in Aspen's room? I gotta get to my baby now,* Shantelle thought.

"Oh, bitch, I plan on takin' everything I want," Deep Voice replied sinisterly.

Deep Voice looked over at the other two men, telling the taller of the two to look for the money. He made sure not to say any names. Tall Man quickly walked out the bathroom, going through all the drawers, finding thousands of dollars in cash. He also came across several pieces of expensive jewelry. Running back into the bathroom, Tall Man showed the others what he'd found.

"Nah, it's way more than that in here. This nigga ballin'. Go check the other rooms in the house and go through everything," Deep Voice informed.

"If all y'all want is money, I got plenty of that shit. I can give y'all whatever y'all want. Y'all can just take the money and leave. I won't say shit or come lookin' for y'all. Just leave. My family ain't got shit to do with nothing." Mario attempted to reason.

"Not the big, bad Mario Billups beggin' for his fuckin life. Nigga, how many times do I have to tell you that you ain't runnin' shit off in this muthafucka? Yo life is in my hands. The life of yo bitch, that's in my hands too. Ain't shit you can do 'bout it, seein' how we caught you in such an unsavory position," Deep Voice uttered.

Reaching down into the tub, he yanked Shantelle out by her arm. She screamed, and Mario attempted to grab her, but Deep Voice was too quick. Shantelle tried to wiggle her way out his grasp, but his strong hold was much too firm. Mario instantly jumped up in an attempt to save his wife; however, he was knocked back down again by the short dude's gun. Mario, however, didn't let that stop him, getting right back up again.

"Take yo fuckin' hands off my muthafuckin' wife!" Mario yelled, blood and spittle flying from his mouth.

Mario didn't give a damn about the gun that was being pointed at him. There was no way these men were going to come into his home and manhandle his wife — his naked wife at that. Mario had a gun inside of his nightstand, next to his bed. He just had to get to it first. He didn't like the way Deep Voice was eyeing his wife's naked body. So, Mario knew that once he did get to his gun, he would be the first person he shot.

"I'm about to put my hand and dick all over her. I told you. I'm here to take everything I want," Deep Voice informed, sending terrified chills throughout Shantelle's body. She was standing there, naked in front of three armed men. She knew her husband would do anything to protect her. However, she also knew he was outnumbered and out armed. She looked over at her husband with frightened eyes, and he looked back at her sympathetically. Mario wanted to assure his wife that everything would be okay and that no harm would come to her. However, he knew he couldn't honestly do that.

ASPEN WOKE up after hearing all the commotion in her home. To Aspen, it sounded like it was coming from her parents' room, but she wasn't entirely sure. She jumped up out of bed and was just about to open her bedroom door when she remembered her father's words. *If anything ever happens and me or yo mama don't come and get you, it's cause we can't. So, you gotta hide and hide good. I don't care what you hear. If it's not me, yo mama, or Cove that come, don't you come out. If someone finds you while you hidin', do yo best to fight them and get away because once they got you, they got you.* Aspen heard her father's words clearly in her head. It was almost as if he was standing next to her.

Aspen quickly crawled under her bed just before her bedroom door opened. She saw huge black boots step inside her room, and she pressed her lips together tightly, trying hard not to make a sound. Her heart pounded, and she placed her hand over her chest, trying to silence the noise. Within seconds, the boots walked out, closing the door behind them.

Aspen could hear her mother screaming and her father yelling with other men. She prayed everything would be okay and that nothing bad would occur. She hoped her parents would come inside her room soon to get her. She needed them to tell her everything was fine, and there was no need to worry. However, when Aspen heard a single gunshot and her mother scream out her father's name right after, she knew something horrible had taken place. Aspen shook in fear as a puddle of urine formed underneath her.

"Noooo! Mario, baby, please get up. Baby, please don't do this. Don't die on me. Please, baby!" Shantelle yelled as she attempted to run to her wounded husband. She'd watched Mario's body jerk from a bullet from the short dude's gun before falling to the floor. However, she was yanked back down, not being able to get to her husband. Deep Voice had a handful of her hair, keeping Shantelle in place. He turned her head to face him before bending down, so they could be eye to eye.

"Bitch, shut the fuck up! I told y'all from the beginning that I'm here to get everything I want. I want to feel what that pussy hittin' foe, and he thought he was gonna stop me from getting that," he spoke.

All Shantelle could think about was Aspen. She knew she had to get to her. Shantelle was certain Aspen had heard the shot, and she knew she was scared. Shantelle looked over at her husband, who had a gunshot wound to the chest. She didn't understand how any of this could happen. She didn't know who these men were or why they were in their house. However, they had indeed come into her home and changed her life forever.

"Go help find the money. I can handle this," Deep Voice told Short Dude.

Short Dude didn't speak, just nodded his head before walking out the bathroom. Shantelle looked Deep Voice in his eyes and knew that if there was ever a chance to get to Aspen, this was it. She was no longer outnumbered, and she remembered the gun her husband kept inside his nightstand. If she could get to it, she would have no problem shooting this man down.

"You 'bout to give me some of that sweet ass pussy," he whispered, pulling his small, skinny penis from his pants, and stroking it.

Shantelle, thinking quick on her feet, quickly kicked Deep

Voice in his crotch, causing him to double over in pain. She took off running, contemplating for a second if she should go to the nightstand and get the gun. Instead, Shantelle ran out the door and toward Aspen's room. She'd almost made it when Deep Voice came from behind her, knocking her hard in the back of her head, causing her to fall to the floor with a loud thud.

Flipping Shantelle over, Deep Voice climbed on top of her, spreading her legs as far as they would go, before entering her. "I told you I was gonna get this pussy," he moaned. Shantelle was so out of it from the blow to her head that she didn't know what was happening. Deep Voice raped her right there on the floor in front of her daughter's bedroom. Aspen heard everything, even the gunshot that ended her mother's life.

CHAPTER TWO

spen didn't crawl from underneath her bed until she was sure the men were gone. She opened her bedroom door and saw her mother's lifeless body lying on the floor. Even her young mind knew her mother was dead. Running down the hall, she grabbed the phone and called the police. She informed the operator that both her parents had been shot. However, she was too young to process that her parents were gone forever. Somehow, in Aspen's head, they would go to the hospital, and everything would be okay — even though she was old enough to know that wasn't reality.

Minutes later, her home was being flooded with police. Everything seemed to be happening in slow motion as strangers taped off her home as a crime scene. One of the officers escorted Aspen out the house and into a squad car until CPS arrived. Cove pulled up a few moments later, being dropped off by her friend's mother. An officer had called her, alerting her of an accident involving her parents, after Aspen had given them her phone number.

Cove screamed out in agony as she watched a body bag being wheeled out on a gurney. Aspen saw her and began yelling her name, hitting the car window to get her attention. Cove looked over and ran to the car, opening the door.

"They shot Mama and Daddy," Aspen cried, falling into Cove's arms.

Cove hugged her sister tightly as they both cried. In one night, their entire world had been altered, and neither of them knew why. They both watched in horror as their other parent was wheeled out in a body bag as well. A car pulled up with a white and blue decal sticker on the driver's side door, and Cove knew it was CPS. Cove watched as an overweight white woman with short, red hair got out the car and walked over to one of the officers. A few moments later, they both walked over to Cove and aspen.

"Hello, my name is Ms. Washington, and you will be coming with me," she spoke.

"Come with you for what?" Cove questioned.

"Both of your parents have been murdered, which makes the two of you wards of the state," she replied coldly.

"Call our Uncle Donté. He's our father's brother. He will come get us," Cove announced.

"Yes, we are aware. His name is Donté Billups. He was

found murdered in his car a few hours earlier," the officer informed.

Just as they thought their hearts couldn't break anymore, they did. Hearing their uncle had also been murdered let them know they had no one left but the two of them. Feeling both heartbroken and defeated, they got into the backseat of Ms. Washington's car, not knowing where they would go from there.

COVE AND ASPEN were in a group home for two days before their mother's sister came to get them. They didn't really know their aunt; Aspen had only seen her twice in her lifetime. She knew her mother was never that close to her sister. So, it seemed odd to the sisters that she would be the one to come and get them.

"You will have to go to court sometime within the next two weeks to get legal custody of the children. Which I'm sure will work in your favor. We would rather put the children in the custody of blood relatives. I think it is wonderful what you're doing, Ms. Atkins," Ms. Washington spoke.

"These are my sister's girls. Of course I was coming to get them." Rochelle spoke in a sweet, calm tone. Walking over to Cove and Aspen, she hugged them tightly. "I'm so sorry. You two babies have been through so much. But Auntie is here now. I know I'm not your mom, but I love you both very much. I promise I will do as much as I can to make your lives as normal as possible," she continued.

Rochelle walked out the building, informing Ms. Washington to follow up with her when she had information about the court date. Cove and Aspen got into the car with their Aunt Rochelle and made their way to her house. There was no more of the huge, comfortable house. Their aunt lived in a three-bedroom apartment in a set of projects in Inkster. She lived there with her two sons, Phillip and Marcus, who were nine and seven. Her boyfriend, Red, also stayed there. Although the apartment wasn't up to the standards of the lifestyle they were used to living, it was clean.

After introducing Cove and Aspen to the rest of the household, Rochelle showed the girls to their new room. The room was small but decorated nicely with pretty shades of pink, purple, and turquoise being the color scheme. It only had space for a set of bunk beds, a dresser, and a small television. However, it would do, seeing how the girls had nowhere else to go.

Cove and Aspen were unable to retrieve any of their clothing from the house after it had become a crime scene. So, Rochelle promised the girls she would take them shopping.

"Y'all hungry? It's some pizza in the kitchen," Red informed.

Both girls declined, opting to go up to their room instead. They were still trying to process the deaths of their parents and uncle, all while having to now live with strangers.

"She seems nice," Aspen said once they were inside their room.

"Yeah, she does, but we don't know her. Daddy told us not to trust nobody we don't know," Cove reminded.

THE NEXT DAY, Rochelle did just as she promised and took the girls shopping. However, there was none of the expensive brand names the girls were used to wearing. Rochelle pulled up at Wal-Mart, giving both Cove and Aspen a budget of a hundred and fifty dollars each. Aspen used to love going to Wal-Mart with her mother when she was alive. Every time they went, Aspen could always pick out whatever toy she wanted. *We never bought clothes from Wal-Mart though,* Aspen thought.

Once they were done shopping, Rochelle took them back home. They'd just pulled up to the apartment when Rochelle's cell phone rang. It was Ms. Washington informing her the court date had been scheduled for next Thursday. She also informed her they would be conducting a home visit the day before. Rochelle happily agreed to everything before ending the call.

"Y'all hungry? I'm bout to go in there and fry some good ass chicken wings," Rochelle stated.

"Aunt Rochelle, has there been any word on who killed Mama and Daddy?" Cove asked.

"I haven't heard anything yet. These police don't care

nothing 'bout some Black lives being lost. They gonna say it was a drug deal gone wrong or something, anything so they don't have to do their jobs and find out what really happened," Rochelle answered.

"Well, when is the funeral? It's been a week, and I haven't heard you say anything about it."

"They didn't have any life insurance, and with us having no family, it's up to me to bury y'all mom. I don't even know how to get in touch with any family y'all dad might have. I don't have any money for a funeral right now. But I'ma save up my money, and we gonna have one soon," Rochelle promised.

Cove nodded her head okay, not liking what she'd heard. Cove headed up to her room with Aspen right behind her. Something didn't feel right to Cove; however, she couldn't put her finger on it. She didn't know anything about funeral costs, but she found it hard to believe that her parents didn't have anything in place in case something happened to them. They were sure to take care of them while they were alive. So, the fact they wouldn't do the same in death was odd to Cove.

"What do you think about what Aunt Rochelle said about Mama and Daddy?" Cove asked.

"What you mean?" Aspen asked.

"Why can't they have a funeral? I know Daddy had money, so where is it? She gave us a hundred and fifty dollars' budget in a damn Wal-Mart." Cove spoke.

"Cove, I don't think she has a lot of money. I mean, look at where she lives. I'm sure Marcus and Phillip wears Wal-Mart clothes too."

"Then why would she come get us if she don't have enough money? We was cool where we was before she came. I could have come up with a way to get us out of that group home myself. I've only saw her a couple times my whole life. She wasn't close to Mama. She wasn't checkin' for us before Mama and Daddy was murdered. So, why she doing it now?"

"Maybe she just didn't want us in that nasty group home. They had rats, Cove, big ones."

"Or maybe it's something else," Cove suggested.

Aspen shrugged Cove off, not thinking anything was unusual. She could see that her aunt didn't have much money, but Aspen could tell she was trying. Aspen took her new clothes out the bags and put them away in her side of the dresser. She knew Cove was upset about the Wal-Mart brand clothes they had to wear. They were not Aspen's style either; however, there was nothing she could do about it. So, she chose to just roll with it. Aspen wanted her parents back. She wanted to go back home to where her loving family once resided. That was all she wanted, and she knew that couldn't happen. So, she didn't care about anything else. She would just have to make the best of her new life.

Walking outside, Aspen looked around for children to play with. She sometimes played with Philip and Marcus; however, they were boys, and Aspen didn't like to play as rough as they did. Walking over to a group of little girls, she introduced herself before joining them in jump rope. It was late August, and the sun was hot as it beamed down on Aspen.

"Where the pool at? It's hot in this sun, and I'm ready to go swimming," Aspen asked, wiping the sweat from her forehead.

"Pool? Ain't no pool around here. Sometimes, Paris mama turns on her water hose, and we run through it and get wet. But she not home," Justice announced.

Justice was a thin, dark-skinned girl, who looked to be the same age as Aspen. She wore a pair of denim shorts with a white t-shirt that had red stains down the front. Her hair was pulled back into a ponytail and looked as though it hadn't been combed in days.

"Dang, it ain't no pool over here? What y'all do for fun when it's hot?" Aspen asked.

"Same thing we doing right now, playing."

Aspen frowned, not wanting to play anymore jump rope. She was becoming too hot. Her aunt didn't have air conditioning like Aspen did in her own home, and the intense August heat was becoming too much. She needed a way to cool off fast. Seeing the disappointment in Aspen's face, Justice motioned for Aspen to follow her, leading Aspen to her apartment. Aspen followed Justice cheerfully, happy she'd met a new friend.

The two girls walked into Justice's apartment and went into the kitchen. Aspen watched as Justice retrieved several empty pop bottles from underneath her sink before filling them with water. Aspen looked on in confusion as she watched Justice fill each bottle one by one.

"Um, what are you doing?" Aspen questioned.

"Ain't no pool or water hose, but we can still have a water fight," Justice replied. "Grab them two bottles and come on," she continued.

Aspen and Justice played for hours, running back into the house every time the bottles became empty. This was the most fun Aspen had in the week since her parents had been murdered. For those hours, she'd forgotten that she was going through the hardest time in her life. She was able to forget that her parents had been murdered, and she was able to just be a child again —_a smiling, cheerful child without a care in the world for those few hours.

"Aspen! Aspen, where are you?" Aspen heard her aunt call her in the midst of her playing.

"I gotta go, but I'll come back tomorrow." Aspen waved before running home.

"I'm right here, Auntie." Aspen ran up, smiling.

"Little girl, where were you, and why are you all wet? Let me tell you something right now. I don't care what you did in yo mama's house. This right here is my house, and you will not leave my house unless you ask me first. Children don't make their own decisions in my house. Children do what adults tell them to do here. Do you understand me?" Rochelle chastised.

Aspen was taken aback by the tone in her aunt's voice.

Aspen didn't think she'd done anything wrong. She'd never had to ask to go outside at her parents' house. She would go outside and play with her friends all day. As long as she was back before the streetlights came on, her parents didn't care. Aspen learned fast that her aunt didn't run her home the same way her parents did.

Rochelle woke Aspen and Cove up early that following Wednesday morning. CPS was due to conduct their home visit before they went to court, and Rochelle wanted everything perfect. She'd spent the day before cleaning the entire house from top to bottom, wanting her home to look and smell clean when the state came to inspect. She didn't want anything to get in the way of her getting custody of her nieces.

"What time are they coming?" Cove asked.

"They will be here at ten, so y'all go take showers, get dressed, and come downstairs," Rochelle replied before walking out the room.

At ten o'clock sharp, Ms. Washington was at Rochelle's house, ready to complete the inspection. She walked through every room of the house, checking everything. She was even sure to check the refrigerator and cabinets to assure there was food in the home.

"Where do the girls sleep?" Ms. Washington questioned.

Rochelle led Ms. Washington up the stairs to the room she'd put together for Cove and Aspen. Ms. Washington was seemingly pleased as she looked over the small room.

"Ms. Atkins, I've seen a lot of homes in this very area, and

I must compliment you on how well you maintain it. The girls have their own space. You have plenty of food. This will work in your favor tremendously. Now, if you would give me and the girls some time to speak alone, this interview will be over," Ms. Washington insisted.

Rochelle walked out the room, leaving the girls alone with Ms. Washington. Rochelle knew there wasn't anything the girls could say to her for them to be removed from her home. So, she didn't mind giving them privacy. She had taken them out of that nasty group home and taken them into her own home. Although it wasn't huge like the house they were used to, it was clean, and they had their own space, unlike the group home they were in. When they were unable to retrieve their clothes from their home, Rochelle had taken them to get new clothes. In her mind, she was trying to show them how good of an aunt she could be.

Ms. Washington was done interviewing the girls and was back in her car within fifteen minutes. Rochelle was due in court at nine the next morning, and she was more than ready. The social worker had all but told her Cove and Aspen were staying with her, and she couldn't have been happier.

"I HEAR by grant full custody of Cove and Aspen Billups to their aunt, Rochelle Atkins," the judge announced before banging his gavel.

When Rochelle made it home with the girls, she decided to

prepare a huge celebration dinner. Aspen asked if she could go outside to play, and Rochelle cheerfully agreed, letting Aspen know not to go too far and to be home before dinner time. Aspen agreed, rushing out the house and off to see Justice. It was determined they would stay with their aunt, so Aspen was happy to have a friend in the neighborhood. The two girls played, taking turns on Justice's skates all afternoon.

CHAPTER THREE

spen and Cove had been living with their aunt for a little over a year, and things had changed drastically since they'd first arrived. Their aunt had become extremely lazy and had stopped cleaning the house. She told both Aspen and Cove that it was their responsibly, seeing how they were staying there rent free. The house was always filled with food; however, neither Aspen nor Cove was allowed to have access to it. Rochelle kept a lock on the fridge and kept everything else in her room. They were only allowed a bowl of cereal for breakfast and a small plate of whatever Rochelle made for dinner. "This food is for my family. Y'all ain't bout to eat everything up from my kids or my man," Rochelle would tell them. There had still been no leads on the people that killed their parents nor had there been a funeral. Anytime Cove or

Aspen asked Rochelle about it, she would yell at them, telling them not to ask her about it anymore.

One day, Cove stayed home sick from school, and Red walked into her room. Cove was asleep underneath her covers when she felt someone sit in her bed. She was confused when she woke up and saw Red scrunching down uncomfortably, sitting on her bottom bunk.

"Hey, Red, you need something?" Cove asked, wiping the sleep from her eyes.

"You in here acting like you sick. I'm already hip on the games y'all teens be playing." Red spoke, taking a sip from his red plastic cup.

Cove could tell he was drunk, and she shook her head before she answered. "I am sick, Red. Why are you in my room?"

"Cause this my house," he shot back, snatching the covers from her body.

"Red, why are you playing so much? I don't feel good. What do you want?" Cove whined.

Red downed the rest of his drink before he answered her. "I want you, and I'm gonna get you."

Cove was confused by his answer as she looked at him, puzzled. Before she could reply, he was on top of her, trying to pull her pajama bottoms off. She screamed as she tried to fight him off, but his force was too strong, and she was no match for him.

"Don't fight it. It's gonna feel good if you just relax and let it happen," Red whispered.

Cove shook in fear as she tried to protect her virginity. She cried and screamed, trying to get him off of her. However, nothing worked, and there was no one at home to hear her screams. Tears fell from her eyes as Red entered her roughly, not giving a damn about the intense pain she was feeling from her hymen being broken.

"Please, Red, don't do this," Cove pleaded weakly. However, her pleas fell on deaf ears as Red continued to pump in and out of her.

"Just relax and enjoy it. I know it feels good. You so fuckin' wet," Red whispered.

Cove laid there in defeat as Red violated her. When it was finally over, Cove couldn't do anything but lay there and cry. Cove was a virgin that was saving her body for the man she knew loved her. Unfortunately, all that was ripped from her the moment Red laid on top of her.

"Go get yourself cleaned up. And if you tell anybody about this, I'ma kill you and yo sister," Red threatened. "I'm not playin' so try me if you want to," he continued before walking out the door.

Cove was terrified to say the least, fearing he was serious. She knew that even if she did tell her aunt, she wouldn't believe her. She knew at that moment that she had to get her and her sister out of their home. Running into the bathroom, Cove locked the door before taking a long, hot shower. She didn't exit the bathroom until her sister and cousins returned home from school.

Cove ran to her room, closing the door behind her. Aspen looked over at her, confused as to why Cove was in such a rush. "What's wrong with you?" Aspen asked.

"We leaving tonight. I don't know where we going or how we gonna get there. We just gotta go tonight," Cove announced in a hushed tone.

"Cove, what are you talking about? We can't leave here and have nowhere to go. We might as well stay here if we just gonna struggle anyway," Aspen reasoned.

"I'm not playin', Aspen. We leaving. As soon as everyone is sleep, we out. I mean that shit." Cove spoke firmly.

Aspen didn't protest any further as she nodded her head, agreeing with her older sister. She could see the fear in her eyes, and although she didn't know what was going on; she knew she was riding with her sister. Aspen watched as Cove got new sheets out the closet and removed the old ones from her bed.

"Is that blood?" Aspen asked, pointing down to Cove's sheets.

"Don't worry 'bout it," Cove answered.

Once Cove was done making her bed, she got back inside it, throwing the covers over her head. She was both heart-broken and physically sick to her stomach. She'd never been violated in that manner before, and all she wanted was her daddy. She knew if her daddy was alive, none of this would be happening. If it did, her father and uncle wouldn't have wasted any time killing him.

"Where you going?" Cove asked Aspen before she walked out the room.

"I'm going to ask Auntie if I can go outside," Aspen answered.

Cove sat up in bed and motioned for Aspen to come closer. "You can go outside, but when you come back in, come right back to this room. And don't tell nobody we leaving tonight," Cove whispered.

Aspen nodded her head before walking out the door. Once outside, she made her way to Justice's house. She wanted to tell her friend she was leaving, but Cove had made it clear she wasn't allowed to tell anyone. This would be the last time she would play with her friend, and it was bittersweet. Although she was definitely going to side with her sister, she didn't want to leave her friend. Walking up to Justice's front door, Aspen knocked and waited for someone to answer. Aspen smiled from ear to ear when a familiar face opened the door.

"Ms. Shanté, what are you doing here? Is Brianna here too? I'm so happy to see you," Aspen cooed.

This was the first time since her parents were murdered that she'd seen anyone from her old neighborhood, and it was a welcomed surprise. Shanté hugged Aspen tightly, excited to see her as well.

"Oh, my God, Aspen, where have you been, and what are you doing here? Me and Brianna didn't know what happened to y'all. Brianna is upstairs playing with Justice. She's gonna be so happy to see you." Shanté beamed.

"Me and Cove moved in with our aunt. She stays right over there" Aspen pointed.

She continued to speak with Shanté until Justice and Brianna came running down the stairs. Both girls were happy to see Aspen, and they hugged her.

"Aspen, I'm so happy! I've been praying every night to find you since you left," Brianna announced.

"Brianna, how do you even now Aspen?" Justice asked.

"This is my best friend. I haven't seen her in over a year. She used to live in this big house with a pool and everything. I used to sleep over there almost every other weekend. Aspen had all the new toys as soon as they came out," Brianna remembered.

"How do y'all know each other?" Aspen asked Brianna.

"Justice is my cousin," Brianna answered.

"What happened to yo big house?" Justice asked.

"Why don't y'all go upstairs and play?" Shanté interrupted, not wanting Aspen to have to answer that question.

Shanté wrote her number down on a piece of paper and handed it to Aspen, letting her know if she needed anything to call her. Aspen agreed before heading off to play with her friends.

. . .

When Aspen walked back into the house a few hours later, she did exactly what Cove informed her to do. Cove was still in bed under the covers but looked up at Aspen when she walked into their room.

"You didn't say anything, did you?" Cove asked.

"No, I didn't," Aspen responded.

"Good. Go downstairs and get you a plate of whatever Aunt Rochelle cooked. Then come right back in this room," Cove ordered. She only had about five hundred dollars. It was the money she had left over from the night her parents were killed. She'd been saving it all this time, knowing she might need it for an emergency. This was, indeed, that emergency.

Cove knew she would be up all night, waiting on everyone to go to sleep, so her and Aspen could leave. When Cove rolled over and saw the clock read two forty-five in the morning, she knew it was time. Cove poked her head out her bedroom door, making sure there were no lights on in the house, before waking Aspen. The two quickly dressed, being sure not to make any noise.

They tiptoed out the room, walking down the hall as their hearts pounded. Both sisters were terrified as they walked down the stairs. The living room was dark, so they didn't see Rochelle sitting on the couch until she turned the light on.

"Where the hell y'all think y'all going?" she asked, frightening the girls, leaving them in shock. "Don't get quiet now. If y'all grown enough to walk out my front door at this hour, then you can tell me where you going," Rochelle continued.

Cove and Aspen stood there, frozen in fear. They were not expecting to be caught by anyone, especially Rochelle. Rochelle stood from the couch, walking over to the girls with her arms folded across her chest. She looked at them both as she waited on one of them to answer. Cove, knowing they'd been caught, decided she was going to tell the truth. *We leavin' anyway, so Red ain't gonna be able to hurt us. Fuck it,* she thought.

"We leaving. We can't stay here no more," Cove answered boldly.

Rochelle took a deep breath, closing her eyes and collecting her thoughts before she replied. "So, y'all thought y'all was just gonna walk out my house in the middle of the night? Y'all little fast asses think y'all grown, huh? Well, tell me this, little girl. Where the fuck were y'all gonna go? You have no money, so what the fuck did you think you were gonna do? Get y'all dumb asses back upstairs before I get mad for real!" Rochelle yelled.

She was already mad at the fact that Red wasn't home, and she didn't need anything adding to her anger. Cove, seeing the frustration in Rochelle's face, moved Aspen behind her before she replied. "We are not stayin' here anymore. We leaving tonight, and there's nothing you can do about it," she reiterated.

"Bitch, if you don't get yo ungrateful ass up them stairs and go to bed. I brought y'all in my home, and this is what y'all do? I should have left y'all dumb asses in that nasty ass group home!" Rochelle yelled.

By this time, both Phillip and Marcus were both out their room and on the stairs, looking at the commotion that was transpiring. They knew how their mother could be, so they knew it was about to be drama in their home.

"Yeah, well, maybe you should have. Maybe then yo nasty ass boyfriend wouldn't have raped me," Cove shot back.

Aspen placed her hand over her mouth, shocked by what her sister revealed. She knew something was wrong by the way she was acting. However, she never thought that rape would be what it was. Aspen stepped from behind Cove and looked into her tear-filled eyes. Anger instantly shot throughout her body, knowing someone had hurt her sister. However, before anyone could say another word, Rochelle pounced on Cove, raining punches on her face, chest, and stomach.

"You lying ass, lil' bitch!"

Punch!

"Ain't nobody raped you!"

Punch!

"I been seein' the way yo fast ass been lookin' at my man since you got here. I thought since you was my niece that you would have a lil' more respect. But I guess I was wrong. You a hoe, just like yo damn mama!" Rochelle screamed.

It took a minute for Aspen's eleven-year-old mind to realize what was happening. However, once she did, she immediately sprang into action, trying to peel Rochelle off Cove. Cove screamed as she attempted to fight back, but she was no match for Rochelle's seasoned fighting skills. With one hand, Rochelle slung Aspen off her and punched Cove in the mouth, busting her lip.

"Mama, stop. You gonna hurt her!" Phillip yelled as he ran down the stairs toward his mother. He tried with all his strength to stop his mother, but his small body held no weight against hers.

Red walked into the house a few moments later, witnessing all the chaos that was erupting, and he didn't know what to do. Instinctively, he ran over to Rochelle and Cove, picking Rochelle up, placing her in a bear hug.

"Rochelle, calm the fuck down! Why the fuck you in here beatin' on that girl like that? Fuck wrong with you?" Red's deep baritone silenced the commotion.

"Nigga, shut the fuck up. You over here defendin' this lil' bitch you fuckin'? You over here fuckin' my niece in my house and guess what, dummy? Her ass walkin' around here sayin' you raped her!" Rochelle yelled.

Red let Rochelle go as he looked over at Cove sinisterly. "Ain't nobody rape this lil' bitch. She damn near threw it at me. I swear, baby. I kept tellin' her no and tried to stop her. But she wanted my dick so bad, she pulled it out my pants," he lied. "Hell, if anybody was getting raped, it was me," Red continued.

"W-what? That is not true, and you know it! I ain't want

you to touch me at all. You came into my room, and I begged you to stop over and over again, and you wouldn't. You raped me, Red!" Cove yelled through her tears.

"Bitch, ain't nobody raped you. You wanted this shit, and we both know it. You know what? Since you wanna lie and say I raped you, you can get the fuck out my house."

"We were leaving anyway," Cove stated, grabbing Aspen's hand, and walking to the door.

"You not takin' Aspen anywhere. You not gonna have her out here with nothin' just cause you wanted to be a hoe. Get the fuck upstairs, Aspen. Cove, you get out!" Rochelle yelled.

Aspen looked over at Cove, not knowing what to do. She could hear the seriousness in Rochelle's voice. However, Cove was clutching her hand tightly, and she couldn't pull away.

"Aspen is not staying here with that pedophile ass mutha-fucka! I'll be damn if Red rapes her too!" Cove shot back.

Rochelle lost it again, slapping Cove in the face so hard she fell to the floor, causing her to let go of Aspen's hand. Red then grabbed Cove up roughly, throwing her onto the porch like day old trash. He slammed the door directly in her face, locking it after. Cove beat on the door, pleading with them to allow Aspen to come with her. She knew she couldn't let her sister stay in that house, afraid of what they might do to her. After about five minutes of her beating and yelling at the door, it finally opened. However, it was neither Aspen nor Rochelle. Red stood on the other side, pointing a gun directly at Cove's head.

"I told you what would happen if you told anyone. I see you didn't believe me. Yo ass lucky she didn't believe you. Now get yo ass from in front of my house with yo loud ass bullshit, or I'll make good on my promise right now." Red spoke through clenched teeth.

Cove shook in fear at the very sight of the gun. She knew at that moment that Red was serious. Something in his eyes told her he would really kill her. She knew she couldn't be any help to her sister if she was dead. So, with that, Cove did the only thing she could do. She left.

CHAPTER FOUR

*I*t was Aspen's fifteenth birthday and the fifth anniversary of her parents' death. She really hadn't celebrated her birthday since the death of her parents. Her born day had become a depressing day for Aspen; however, this year was going to be different. Shanté had planned an entire day for Aspen, Brianna, and Justice. Rochelle had even agreed to let her go, and Aspen was excited. She'd gotten up at eight that morning and gotten dressed. Shanté wasn't going to pick them up until ten. However, Aspen was at Justice's house by nine-thirty.

"Aww, shit, it's the birthday girl!" Justice announced when Aspen walked inside. "Happy birthday, bestie," Justice continued.

"Thank you." Aspen smiled.

"You ready to get yo day started? It's about to be so much fun. Auntie Shanté always puts together the best shit."

"Yeah, I'm ready. I actually can't wait. This gonna be the first time I celebrated my birthday in five years," Aspen replied.

Justice was right. Shanté's plans were the best. Aspen hadn't had a day like this since her mother was still alive. It reminded her of how they used to spend their Saturday mornings. They went to the spa where they got massages and facials. The entire scene was relaxing, and Aspen enjoyed every moment of being pampered. Once they were finished at the spa, they made their way to the salon. Shanté had made them all appointments to get their hair and nails done. This was the first time in five years that Aspen's hair had any type of professional attention, and it was much needed. After a hot oil treatment and a Brazilian blowout, Aspen's hair was down her back.

"Thank you so much, Ms. Shanté. This has been the best day I've had in a long time," Aspen confessed.

"I'm glad I'm making your day special, but we're nowhere near done yet," Shanté replied.

When they pulled into the parking lot of Sommerset Mall, Aspen couldn't do anything else but smile. She used to walk this mall with her mother and sister every Saturday, buying anything they wanted. It brought back so many happy memories of her mother, warming Aspen's heart.

"Okay, girls, we need to get nice dresses and shoes for dinner tonight. And Aspen, since it's your day, you can get two outfits and another pair of shoes from any store you want." Shanté smiled.

They spent about two hours in the mall until everyone found what they needed. Aspen picked out a royal blue dress that stopped about an inch above her knees. The top was fitting and hugged her waist before flaring out at the bottom. She paired it with a pair of royal blue, one-inch heels. Justice went with a purple dress, while Brianna chose a pink one. Shanté kept it classy with all black. Once they were all done shopping, Shanté took them back to her house to get dressed.

"Okay, we have reservations in two hours. Let's all get cute so we can have some more fun." Shanté beamed.

Aspen couldn't have been more thankful for the day Shanté put together for her. She felt special for the first time in years. As she placed the dress on her body, she loved the way the expensive fabric felt on her skin. It had been years since she'd been in anything other than Wal-Mart clothes, and she welcomed the change. After placing some mascara on her lashes and a bit of gloss on her lips, Aspen was ready.

"You look so beautiful," Shanté complimented once Aspen walked into the living room.

"Thank you," Aspen cooed.

"Before we head to dinner, Brianna and I have one more gift for you," Shanté announced.

"Ms. Shanté, you have done so much for me already."

"And now we have one more gift," Brianna said, handing Aspen a gold gift bag.

Aspen smiled, taking the bag from Brianna. Reaching into the bag, she pulled out two blue Tiffany boxes. A huge smile spread across her face when she realized the store the boxes were from. She opened the boxes to see a necklace in one and a pair of earrings in the other. She was so happy that she hugged both Brianna and Shanté, thankful for her gifts.

"These are beautiful. Thank y'all so much."

"You're welcome, Aspen. You deserve every moment of this day. Now, we gotta get going before we miss our reservations." Shanté spoke.

They pulled up in the parking lot of Andiamo's and walked inside. Shanté walked up to the hostess, letting her know they had reservations for five. Once they were seated at their table, Aspen asked who the other place belonged to. Shanté smiled, telling Aspen to look behind her. When Aspen turned around, tears filled her eyes as she stood to her feet.

"Happy birthday, baby sis." Cove smiled as she embraced her sister.

"Cove, oh, my God, I've missed you so much. Where have you been?"

"I missed you too, Aspen. You look so beautiful. You're

all grown up now," Cove complimented, taking a step back to admire her sister.

"Thank you. You look beautiful too, Cove," Aspen replied, taking her seat as Cove took the empty seat alongside her.

Aspen hadn't seen her sister in four years, and she couldn't stop crying as she looked at her. She couldn't believe how much she'd changed. There were no more Wal-Mart clothes for her. Cove sat there in designer clothes from head to toe. They all set around the table celebrating Aspen, sharing laughs the two sisters hadn't had in years. Before they left the restaurant, Cove asked Aspen to follow her back to her car.

"I got a few birthday gifts for you. I also wanted to talk to you alone," Cove informed.

The two of them got into Cove's all white G-wagon, and she handed Aspen a pink envelope. Aspen opened it to see it was filled with bills. "It's ten thousand dollars. Don't tell nobody you got it either," Cove informed.

"Oh, my God! Thank you so much, sistah!" Aspen screamed, excited about the money.

Cove also handed Aspen two gift boxes. Aspen opened the first one to see a phone inside. Cove had been forced to have no contact with her sister for years, and Cove had had enough of it. So, Cove knew that if she wanted to speak with her whenever she wanted, she would have to buy Aspen a phone. The next box Aspen opened housed a gun. Aspen's mouth dropped open as she looked at her sister, confused.

"Aspen, I'm about to ask you something that I need for you to be completely truthful about," Cove uttered.

"Okay, What's up?"

"Has Red ever tried to touch you or done anything to hurt you?"

"No, he hasn't done anything to me, not like that. He just been the same old Red," Aspen replied.

"Look, if that muthafucka tries anything with you, I want you to shoot his ass. Don't let him get you. I wish I had a gun that day he raped me. If I did, you wouldn't even have to worry about it. But you gonna have to protect yoself while you there. I'm gonna be getting my own place in a couple weeks, and you coming to stay with me."

"I can come stay with you? Cove, I can't wait. It's so depressing in that house. And without you there, I feel so alone." Aspen spoke honestly.

Cove hated she had to leave her sister at their aunt's house, but she had no choice. She was only sixteen at the time and being threatened at gun point by Red scared her. She did try to come back and get Aspen one other time after that. It was about a year after she'd left. The moment she stepped onto the porch, Red opened the door, shooting. Cove barely made it out with her life, and she knew she could never step foot back at that house again. She knew she would have to get Aspen out the house a different way.

"Hell yeah you are. I just need two weeks then it's gonna be me and you, lil' sis."

Aspen smiled. The entire day had been perfect, and she had Shanté to thank for it all. Not only had Shanté showed her a great time by showing her love she hadn't felt in years, but she had also reunited her with her sister. That was the best gift she could have gotten. Before Aspen got out of Cove's car, Cove made sure to save her number into Aspen's new phone.

ASPEN WALKED BACK into her aunt's house that night on cloud nine. She took all of her gifts up to her room, being sure to hide the money and gun first, before doing anything else.

"I see that lady bought you a lot of gifts. You must have had a good time." Rochelle spoke, walking into Aspen's room.

"Yeah, Ms. Shanté is so sweet. We went to a spa, got our hair and nails done, and everything. I had so much fun," Aspen gushed.

"Well, that's good. Somebody had to buy yo ass something cause I damn sure wasn't gonna waste none of my money on you," Rochelle shot.

Aspen recoiled, not understanding the hatred that was coming from her aunt. She always made it her business to let Aspen know she didn't like her, and Aspen couldn't understand why. *She could have kept that shit to herself,* Aspen thought.

"Do something with that hair and take off that dress. You look like a fuckin' slut. If you think you bout to be the next bitch in my house eye fuckin' my man, you got another thing comin'. I'll beat the fuck outta you just like I did yo sista," Rochelle continued.

Red walked past the door, popping his head in before Aspen could reply. He smiled, licking his lips as he looked at Aspen. He'd never seen her look so beautiful, and his dick stiffened at the sight of her.

"Happy birthday, Aspen," he said, handing Aspen a birthday card.

"Thank you." Aspen spoke, opening the card.

"You betta remember what I said," Rochelle reiterated before walking out the room.

"Don't pay her no mind. It's yo day, and you look beautiful in that dress," Red complimented.

"Thank you."

Aspen opened the card to find a hundred dollars inside. If her sister hadn't just handed her ten thousand dollars an hour before, she would be more enthused about the gift. However, Aspen knew Red's true intentions for giving her the gift, so she placed the card and money down on her dresser and thanked him.

"You're welcome, and you really do look beautiful." Red spoke before walking out her room, closing the door behind him.

Aspen put the rest of her gifts away before wrapping her hair, placing a scarf over it. She made her way to the bathroom to take a shower. When she walked back into her room, she was surprised to see Red standing there with two drinks in his hand.

"I think you old enough to have a birthday drink with me," Red stated.

"Red, get out my room. I'm not having drinks with you. I'm fifteen," Aspen replied.

"Man, you right. I don't know what I was thinking. You probably think I'ma say something to Rochelle if you have a drink with me, huh? I ain't gonna say shit, Aspen," he whispered.

"Red, please get out. I don't drink, and I'm tired. I just wanna go to sleep. Red, please, I've had a long day."

Red stood there, staring at Aspen for several seconds, causing her to feel uneasy. The gun Cove had given to her was under her mattress on the other side of the room. Her heart dropped for a second until Red walked out of her room. Aspen blew out a breath of relief, closing her door behind Red. She immediately took the gun from underneath the bed, placing it under her pillow.

ASPEN ONLY HAD a week left before she was moving in with Cove. They'd spoken every day since they'd gotten back in touch with each other, and Aspen was happy to have her sister back in her life. Cove informed Aspen that she could decorate her room however she wanted, and Aspen couldn't wait. Aspen had just taken a shower and gotten in bed for the night when Red walked into her room. Aspen could tell he was drunk by the way he stumbled over to her bed.

"Why you going to sleep so early?" Red slurred.

"Because I'm tired. Can you get out my room?"

Aspen slid her hand under her pillow to assure she had easy access to her gun if need be. Red sat at the edge of Aspen's bed and took a sip from his cup before speaking again.

"Why you be talkin' to me like that? I came in here to chill with you. Ain't nobody else home for me to chill with. Yo auntie and the boys ain't here. They down at Rochelle's hood rat ass friend's house, probably talkin' shit 'bout a nigga right now. Ain't no telling when they gon' be home. I need somebody to chill with," Red responded drunkenly.

"Red, just get out my room. You drunk, and I don't have time for this. You already know Auntie Rochelle not gonna like you being in my room."

"That bitch ain't here. I ain't thinkin' about her, and you shouldn't be either. She don't even like you. The only reason she let you and yo sister stay here is so she could get dem checks for y'all," Red revealed, taking another sip from his glass.

Aspen knew enough to know a drunken tongue spoke a sober mind, so she decided to get all the information she could from Red. "What money?" she asked.

"Rochelle gets money every month from the state for you.

She was getting it for Cove too, even after she left. Shit stopped when she turned eighteen though," Red informed.

Red finished the rest of his drink, and it had him seeing double. When he looked over at Aspen this time, his dick stiffened, and he knew he wanted her. Red leaned in and tried to kiss Aspen, but she turned away.

"Red, what the hell are you doing?"

"I'm getting what I want, and what I want is you. And you gonna give it to me. You do what Rochelle tells you, and she was the one who set up yo parents' murders. Now you 'bout to listen to me and get my dick wet." Red spoke.

His word shocked Aspen so badly she zoned out. *Rochelle had my mama and daddy killed? Why would she do that? That was her sister, and she had her killed?* Aspen was in such a deep trance that she didn't even realize Red was on top of her until he already had her pants down.

"Red, get the fuck off me!" Aspen yelled.

"Hell nah, this pussy 'bout to be mine."

It was that right there. The way Red said the word "pussy" brought Aspen right back to her tenth birthday. She could hear her mother being raped outside her bedroom door. She would never forget the raunchy way the man had said that exact word. *It was Red. He was the muthafucka that came into my house that night and killed Mama and Daddy.*

The moment the revelation entered Aspen's head, she pulled her gun from under her pillow, pointing it to Red's head before firing. She ended his life before he even knew what was happening.

Blood and brain matter spattered all over her face, walls, and bed. It didn't matter to her because she would not be staying at that house tonight. She walked down the stairs and sat on the couch, waiting on Rochelle to come back home. Thirty minutes later, Rochelle was walking into the house. Aspen was glad she didn't have the boys with her; however, in the state she was in, it probably wouldn't have mattered anyway.

"Girl, what the hell is all over yo face? Is Red here?" Rochelle asked, as she walked into her living room.

Aspen didn't say a word as she looked at Rochelle, trying to gather her thoughts. Rochelle walked closer to Aspen before speaking again. "Did you fuckin' hear me, little girl? Where is Red, and what the fuck is that all over you?"

"I'm gonna ask you this one time only. It's in yo best interest to tell the truth. Why the fuck did you have my parents killed?" Aspen spoke in a no-nonsense tone.

"W-what the fuck are you talkin' 'bout? Don't ask me no stupid ass question like that. Fuck wrong with you?"

"If I ask you again, you not gonna like what I do after that," Aspen whispered.

Rochelle burst out into laughter, not taking Aspen seriously at all. She knew she was all bark and no bite, so Rochelle decided to call her bluff.

"Look, lil bitch, ever since yo birthday, you been smellin'

yoself. If you askin' if I had yo parents killed, then you already know I did. They had it comin'. How you got all that money and don't take care of yo family? Yo mama thought she was the shit cause she caught a baller, but she wasn't. That bitch wasn't shit, and she died like the trash she was. At the end, I got all the money she would never share with me. I got her kids too and got paid real good for havin' y'all. So, I ended up winnin' anyway. You wanted to know the truth, there you go, now what the fuck you gonna do about it?" Rochelle spoke, not giving a damn about Aspen finding out anymore. Rochelle knew she held all the power, and she dared Aspen to try to challenge her.

Aspen didn't say a word as she stood to her feet and held up her gun. Rochelle stood there in shock as she looked down the barrel of the gun. Aspen had heard all she needed to hear to figure out what her next move was going to be.

"Aspen, please put the gun down. I was just talking shit. You know I would never kill my sister," Rochelle pleaded.

Aspen laughed sinisterly as she looked at Rochelle. "Bitch, everything you just said was true. Yo drunk ass boyfriend already told me the truth before he tried to rape me. He upstairs dead, and now, you bout to be right with him. My mama and daddy bout to fuck y'all up in the afterlife," Aspen uttered before raining shots down on Rochelle.

"Hello?" Cove answered the phone sleepily.

"Cove, I need you to come to the house. I just did something bad." Aspen spoke into the phone.

Cove, already knowing Aspen had used the gun she'd given her, told Aspen to get in the shower and wash every inch of her body before letting her know she was on her way. Aspen's heart beat fast as she walked back into her room to get a change of clothes. Seeing Red lying dead on her bed sent chills throughout her body. She was only fifteen and had just killed two people.

CHAPTER FIVE

ove arrived at the house, not expecting to see the scene she saw when she stepped into the living room. She looked at her aunt lying there on the floor. Blood was everywhere — all over the walls, furniture, and floor. Rochelle had so many bullet holes inside her face that she was unrecognizable.

"Aspen, I thought you were gonna tell me you shot Red for trying to rape you. What the hell happened here?" Cove asked, looking down at the bloody mess.

"I did. I killed him too. He's upstairs in my bedroom. They killed Mama and Daddy," Aspen whispered.

"What?! How do you know that?" Cove questioned, turning to look at Aspen in disbelief.

"They told me. Red was one of them men that came into the house that night. He was the one that raped Mama and killed her. And Rochelle put it all together. She set up her own sister," Aspen revealed.

Cove broke down in tears at the revelation. Everything was starting to make sense. Rochelle had never given her parents a funeral because she was their killer. She never had any information to give them because she was covering for herself. Cove could have kicked herself for not seeing this before now.

"They was getting money for us living with them every month, and all the money Mama and Daddy had, they took that too," Aspen continued.

Cove had heard enough; her sister had killed her parents' murderers. She'd gotten street justice for them at the young age of fifteen, so Cove knew what she had to do next.

"Go get yo stuff. Make sure you get the gun too," Cove ordered.

Aspen did as she was told, running up to her room and grabbing everything she'd gotten for her birthday. She walked over to her bed and quickly got her money that was underneath, careful not to touch Red's body. Once she had everything, she ran back downstairs, handing Cove the gun.

"Give me yo stuff and you go out the back door. I'll go out the front and meet you at the end of the street. I don't want nobody seeing you." Cove spoke.

Aspen nodded her head okay and rushed out the back door while Cove went out the front. They met at the end of the street, and Cove drove Aspen back to the city. They pulled up to a brick home about twenty minutes later.

"Whose house is this?" Aspen asked.

"It's mine. I thought I would be able to get more furniture before you moved in, but shit ain't work out like that. Come on. Let's take your stuff inside and you can pick what room you want."

Aspen picked her room, and Cove gave Aspen a set of pajamas to change into, letting Aspen know to come to the living room when she was done. Cove's mind was running on a thousand; however, she needed to make sure her little sister was okay. She hated this for her sister and wanted to do anything she could to make it better.

Aspen walked into the living room and sat down next to her sister on the couch. She looked over at Cove, eyes filled with tears. "Why did she have to be so jealous of Mama that she killed her?" Aspen cried. Cove didn't have an answer to Aspen's question, so she wrapped her arms around Aspen, bringing her in for a tight embrace.

The two sisters stayed up for hours, sharing fond memories of their parents. It was five in the morning by the time Aspen went upstairs to her new bedroom. It wasn't decorated yet; it didn't have anything inside but a queen-sized bed and a television, which was mounted on the wall. However, she knew her sister would take her to fill the room with whatever she wanted to put inside it.

. . .

Aspen woke up around two that afternoon after getting some of the best sleep she'd had in years. She walked to Cove's room and saw she wasn't inside. Feeling hunger pains in her stomach, Aspen walked down to the kitchen. Seeing the note that hung on the fridge, she grabbed it and began reading.

Aspen, my beautiful baby sister. I love you so much. The only thing I've ever wanted from the time Mama and Daddy died was to take care of you.

I want you to have a good life, free from worry and heartache. And so far, all you've had is worry and heartache. So, I'm doing the only thing I can do to make sure you live the way you deserve to. I want you to know that I have thought this over, and this was the only option. Don't worry about nothing and don't blame yoself for shit. This was my decision, and I'm good with it.

I turned myself in for Red and Rochelle's murders. Don't come see me. I'll be okay and so will you. In my nightstand in my bedroom is twenty thousand dollars. The rent for the house is paid up for the next five years. The utilities are paid up for the next six months. Nothing is in my name, so you ain't gotta worry bout nobody taking it away from you. The money you have should cover you for a minute. If you need anything, Shanté will help you. You can trust her, Brianna, and Justice too. They all really have your back. I hope in time you will forgive me for leaving you again.

Love always and forever,
Cove.

. . .

ASPEN'S EYES filled with tears as she read the letter. She couldn't believe she was alone again. She had been the one to kill Red and Rochelle, and now, her sister would be the one to pay the price for her actions. Aspen felt alone and helpless. She was only fifteen years old and didn't know the first thing about being an adult or paying bills. Here she was, in this house that was now hers, and she was all alone.

Her appetite was now gone as she made her way up to Cove's room and got into her bed and cried. Just when she thought things were better, here she was, still with no family and all alone. Aspen stayed in Cove's bed for the rest of the day, crying into her pillow.

That next morning, Aspen woke up ready to start the first day of the rest of her life. She had been dealt a bad hand in life; however, she would be damned if she let that shit define her. There was no way she would let her sister lose her freedom in vain. Walking to the bathroom, Aspen took a shower before doing her hair and dressing for the day.

Once she finally got to her phone, she saw she had over twenty missed calls from both Justice and Brianna. She decided against calling them back for now. She knew by now the police had been at her aunt's house, and Justice wanted to know what was going on. She wasn't ready to speak on it just yet. So, she decided she wouldn't call them until she was.

Walking back into Cove's bedroom, she opened her nightstand to see the money Cove had told her about. Adding that to the money Cove had given her for her birthday, she had thirty thousand dollars. It sounded like a lot to her fifteen-year-old mind, but Aspen didn't know how much the utilities would be once she had to start paying them in six months. Cove had also left Aspen the keys to her Mercedes truck. However, Aspen didn't know how to drive. So, she knew she would have to be taught. With that, Aspen googled the Michigan driver's handbook and began reading, deciding that she would ask Ms. Shanté to give her driving lessons.

IT HAD BEEN two days since Cove had turned herself in, and Aspen was finally ready to talk to her friends. She called Brianna and asked her if Ms. Shanté could bring her and Justice to where she was. Brianna agreed, and an hour later, they were walking through the door with Ms. Shanté right behind them.

"Oh, my God, Aspen, are you okay?" Shanté asked, bringing Aspen in for a hug. "Justice said there was about a half dozen police cars at yo aunt's house. And when we found out her and her boyfriend had been murdered and we couldn't find you, I was so worried," she continued.

"Yeah, I'm okay," Aspen replied.

"Whose house is this?" Shanté asked.

"It's mine. Cove left it to me before she turned herself in," Aspen explained.

"Turned herself in for what?" Brianna asked.

"She turned herself in for killing Red and Rochelle," Aspen revealed.

"What? Cove killed them?" Brianna questioned.

Aspen didn't say a word as she hung her head low. She knew her sister didn't kill anyone. However, she'd said she did in order to save Aspen.

"Wait, so yo sister left you a whole house?" Justice asked, looking around in amazement.

"Yeah, she did and a car too. Ms. Shanté, can you teach me how to drive?" Aspen asked.

"Yeah, I got you. But I'm not sure about you staying here all alone. How will you make money to pay the bills?" Shanté questioned.

"The bills are paid for now, and she left me some money to start paying them when they're due again. I might need your help with that as well."

Shanté nodded, letting Aspen know she would help with whatever she needed her to. Shanté loved Aspen like her own daughter, so there was nothing she wouldn't do for her. "Aspen, what happened at Rochelle's house? Why did Cove kill them?" Shanté asked.

"Because they were hurting us for years. Red tried to rape me that night and told us him and Rochelle killed our parents. Cove lost it after that. Now they dead and she in jail," Aspen revealed, telling a half truth.

"Hurtin' you? Aspen, why didn't you say anything? You

could have stayed with me. You would have never had to stay there if I knew they were hurtin' you. Friend, why didn't you tell me?" Justice spoke, hurt all over her tone. She loved Aspen and would have never allowed anyone to hurt her.

"Thanks, Jay, but sometimes the only way out of something is through it. I had to stay there. If I didn't, I might not have ever found out they killed my parents," Aspen replied.

Justice nodded her head in understanding, admiring her friend's high spirts in her time of tribulation. Even with Aspen standing there smiling, she knew her heart was heavy. So, without another word, Justice walked over and hugged her friend tightly.

"Don't worry. You gonna be good, Aspen. We got you. How about we order some Chinese food and have a little girls' day in? Y'all can watch some movies or something. Then, tomorrow, I'll start teaching you how to drive. What you think?" Shanté suggested.

"Yeah, that sounds good," Aspen replied.

Shanté placed the order for the girls' food, leaving the money on the counter before leaving out to go pack Brianna and Justice an overnight bag. The three friends sat in Aspen's living room, flipping through the channels on the TV. She was happy to have her friends there with her, and the girls spent the rest of the night eating food and watching movies.

CHAPTER SIX

It had been two years since Aspen had been on her own, and she had adapted nicely. She'd stopped going to school out of fear the state was looking for her as a runaway. So, she began teaching herself. She would read several books a month because she knew knowledge was power. She still had most of the money Cove left her and was doing well considering everything she'd been through.

Cove had been sentenced to fifteen years for the murders of Red and Rochelle. She would be eligible for parole after ten years due to the reasons of the crime. Cove didn't want Aspen to come and see her in prison; however, she wrote her twice a week. Cove also received visits from Shanté once a month, so Aspen knew she was doing okay. Things were starting to come together for Aspen, and she was starting to feel good about life.

Brianna and Justice were at her house almost every day, and she'd even gotten a boyfriend by the name of Moe. Moe was a twenty-year-old she'd met about a year ago when she was doing a little shopping at Sommerset. He walked up to her, introducing himself, and they'd been joined at the hip ever since. Moe stood six foot two inches tall. He was rather skinny however, had started going to the gym to build his muscle. His dark chocolate skin was what really attracted Aspen to him. She'd not seen skin that smooth since her father, and it instantly caught her attention. He helped her out a lot, paying her bills and putting food in her house, so she could save her money.

Aspen was sitting on the couch, flipping through Netflix, when she heard Moe come through the door.

"Baby, go get dressed. We bout to go out and celebrate," Moe yelled, walking over to the couch, grabbing Aspen. He picked her up and hugged her excitedly.

"What are we celebrating?" Aspen asked, confused.

"I just got a good ass deal on some kilos that's gonna set us up real nice. Once this shit is sold, we gonna be lookin' at seven figures. Shit, with money like that, we can do whatever we want," Moe informed.

Aspen smiled, seeing how happy her man was. Moe always did whatever he could to put a smile on Aspen's face so seeing him with a smile on his warmed Aspen's heart. "I'm so proud of you, baby."

Aspen rushed to the bathroom and began getting dressed.

She knew Moe never did anything small, so she knew she would have to dress to the nines for whatever they did. She dressed in a black Chanel dress with the heels and purse to match. Her jewelry was Fendi, and her fragrance of choice was Dior. She placed huge curls in her hair and feathered them over her face. Once she applied red lipstick, she was ready to go.

"Damn, baby, you look good as hell," Moe complimented.

Moe matched Aspen's fly with his black Balmain ensemble. The YSL cologne he wore was Aspen's favorite, and she instantly became moist when the scent invaded her nostrils. They got into Moe's Range Rover and made their way downtown. Aspen felt her best when she was with Moe, and she was happy he'd come into her life.

Aspen smiled when they entered the parking structure for the Renaissance center, knowing they were going to Forty-Two Degrees North. This would be her first time at the restaurant, and she was excited because she'd heard good things about it.

"This is so nice, babe," Aspen cooed, looking around at the beautiful scenery.

"Get used to it, baby. It's only up from here. I'm gonna give you the world, baby. Just you watch."

Aspen smiled, knowing Moe was telling the truth. She knew Moe loved her and would do anything for her. She loved him too and was grateful he'd come into her life. Being with Moe was like a breath of fresh air. He showed her the type of love she knew she deserved. Moe didn't half step with Aspen, and she was smitten. After dinner, they went back to Aspen's house for a few drinks. They were both under twenty-one, so they couldn't order alcohol at the restaurant. However, they toasted to their newly found wealth as soon as they got home. They spent the rest of the night celebrating by making love under candlelight.

The next morning, Aspen woke up to find a note and money left on her nightstand. Moe stated in the note that he had to leave out early to handle some business. He also told her he'd left the money for her to go shopping with her girls, so she could stay occupied while he was away. Aspen jumped out of bed and went to the bathroom to shower. After dressing in a red and white oversized Balenciaga sweater and a pair of thigh high white boots, Aspen placed a call to Brianna.

"What up doe?" Brianna answered.

"What you doin'? You wanna hit up Sommerset?" Aspen asked.

"You know I ain't never gonna turn down a trip to the mall. Lemme call Justice and see if she wanna roll with us."

"Cool, I'm 'bout to pull up on you in a few." Aspen spoke.

Aspen ended the call, walking out of her house and getting into her G-wagon. She was at Brianna's house within fifteen minutes. Aspen walked inside to say her hellos to Shanté before her and Brianna headed off to pick up Justice.

The group of three made it to the mall, going in store after store and trying on all the items they liked until they worked up an appetite. Making their way to the food court, they got their food and all sat around the table to eat.

"What we doin' this weekend, y'all?" Brianna asked, dipping a fry into a pile of ketchup.

"Shit, I hear Dominque havin' a party," Justice suggested.

"Oh, yeah, I did hear something about that. We can hit that up if y'all want to. You down, Aspen?" Brianna asked.

"Yeah, I guess so. I really don't know Dominque like that, but if y'all wanna go, we can," Aspen stated.

"Cool, I'ma buy myself a new outfit. I need to be lookin' good. I already know it's gonna be some fine ass niggas there. I'm tryin' to get boo'd with a baller like you, Aspen," Justice joked. The three friends laughed, finishing their food. When they were done eating, the three of them finished shopping, finding everything they needed to look good at the party.

When Aspen finally made it back home after spending hours with her friends, she was surprised to see that Moe wasn't back yet. Walking into her bathroom, Aspen ran herself a bubble bath before pouring herself a glass of wine. She wanted to relax and unwind from her long day of shopping. Once out the tub, she decided to call Moe to see if he was coming over. When he didn't answer, Aspen assumed he wasn't coming, and she went on about her night, watching Netflix until she fell asleep.

.   .   .

Dominque's basement was packed with people from wall to wall. The music was bumping, and everyone was having a good time. Aspen stood against the wall, sipping from a red plastic cup while she bobbed her head to the beat. Brianna was in the middle of the dance floor, popping her shit like her life depended on it, while Justice stood at the food table, piling chicken wings onto her plate.

"Bitch, the entire hood at this party. This shit lit as fuck, and these wings good as hell too," Justice yelled over the music as she joined Aspen.

"Yeah, everybody here. I'm 'bout to join Bri on the dance floor. I can't let her have all the fun," Aspen joked.

"You go right ahead. I'm 'bout to finish my wings."

Aspen walked over to the dance floor, watching as party-goers crowded around Brianna, forming a circle. The house music blared though the speakers as the entire party watched Brianna's footwork. The entire crowd hyped her up as they yelled, "Uh oh," every time DJ Godfather did. When the song changed and DJ Assault began chanting "Gel-n-Weave," not even Aspen could hold back her Jit, joining Brianna and showing off her footwork as well. House music never got old in the city of Detroit, and the Jit reigned supreme against any city's dance moves.

Both Aspen and Brianna had worked up a sweat by the end of the song and decided to head to the drink table. Justice ran up to them as soon as she saw them, grabbing Aspen's hand, forcing Aspen to walk with her.

"Girl, what you doing? I need something to drink. I know you seen me out there giggin'. Shit, a bitch is thirsty." Aspen spoke.

"Bitch, fuck all that. I just seen Moe all hugged up and kissin' all over Dominque," Justice informed.

"Moe? My man Moe? Nah, Justice, ain't no way you see Moe with no damn Dominque. My man would never do no shit like that."

Justice didn't say another word as she led Aspen up the stairs and out the front door. There, leaning against his hunter green Range Rover, was Moe with Dominque standing in front of him. He had his arms around her waist as they stood there talking.

"Bitch, what you wanna do? Cause I'm down for whatever," Justice stated, letting her friend know she would stand beside her.

Aspen couldn't speak. She could only stand there as her heart broke into pieces. Aspen would have never imagined Moe would do anything to hurt her, especially something like this. She watched in shock as Moe bent down and kissed Dominque on the lips. Aspen's eyes burned as tears threatened to fall.

"Bitch, do you hear me? What you wanna do?" Justice reiterated. "I know you ain't 'bout to let this nigga play in yo face like that? I say we walk over there and see what's up," Justice continued.

Aspen didn't know what to do as she watched on in hurt.

Part of her wanted to break down into tears as she watched the man she loved show love to another woman. While the other part of her wanted to run up and beat the hell out of them both. After several seconds of going back and forth with herself, Aspen finally decided to confront Moe.

"What up doe?" Aspen greeted, looking directly at Moe. She saw the shocked look on his face and knew he wasn't expecting to see her at the party. "What you got going on here?" Aspen continued.

"Aspen? What are you doing here?" Moe asked in evident confusion. He quickly took his arm from around Dominque's body as he stared at Aspen. He knew he was caught red handed. However, in true nigga fashion, he was going to attempt to talk his way out of the situation. "Aspen, I know…" Before he could finish speaking, Dominque chimed in.

"Listen, um, I'm glad you came to my party and everything. But that don't mean you can just interrupt me while I'm having a conversation with my man. We in the middle of some deep shit right now. So, if you could please excuse us."

"Bitch, this is not yo man," Justice informed, pointing to Moe.

"I got his baby growing inside me, so whose man is he?" Dominque spoke, stepping away from Moe and closer to Justice.

Aspen saw red as Dominque stood there talking cash shit. Anger shot through her body, and she couldn't stop herself when she lunged at Dominque, punching her directly in her face. Moe grabbed Aspen the moment he saw her fist connect with Dominque's face, holding her tightly so she couldn't hurt Dominque any further.

"Aspen, just please calm down and let me explain," Moe whispered in Aspen's ear so only she could hear him.

"Explain what? You wanna explain to me how you been cheatin' on me, got another bitch pregnant? You been in my face, tellin' me you love me and shit. All the while, you makin' a whole family with the next bitch. Fuck you, Moe. You ain't shit!" Aspen screamed, pulling herself from Moe's grasp.

"Moe, what the fuck is this bitch talkin' about?" Dominque questioned.

Moe looked into the eyes of both of his women as they stood there waiting on him to answer their questions. He didn't know what to say. He'd been caught red handed, trying to have his cake and eat it too. He truly did love Aspen. That was the one thing he hadn't lied about. However, he loved Dominque as well, and she was the one carrying his child. With Dominque being pregnant, he didn't want to put any stress on her that could potentially harm their unborn child.

"Dominque, why don't you go sit in my car while I talk to Aspen?" Moe suggested.

"Sit in yo car? Fuck you mean? Tell that bitch it's over and let's go back inside," Dominque countered.

Moe was caught between a rock and a hard place. He didn't want to hurt Aspen, but he knew he couldn't choose her over his child's mother. He never meant to take things this far. When he first met Aspen, he thought he could just fuck her a few times and leave her alone. Moe wasn't looking for a relationship because he was already in one with Dominque. However, Aspen treated him like a king, so the selfish side of him wanted to keep her around. The very day he decided he wanted to make a choice and only be with Aspen was the same day Dominque told him she was pregnant. He knew then he couldn't fully be with Aspen.

"Bitch, I don't know what you thought, but this nigga ain't goin' nowhere. Not until he explains to my best friend what the fuck is going on," Justice chimed in, seeing the hurt all over Aspen's face.

"No, bitch, I don't know what you thought. My man don't owe no explanation to no other bitch. It's clear that he don't want her ass cause if he did then he wouldn't be with me. Let me give y'all dumb asses some advice. A nigga gonna always pick his family over a side bitch any day."

With that comment, Aspen was done. She was no one's side bitch. Moe had played the both of them. The only difference was Dominque had gotten pregnant. She wasn't about to stand there and listen to anymore. Aspen no longer cared what Moe did with Dominque or anyone else for that matter. Aspen had never had her heart broken by a man before, so the feeling was new to her. Fighting the tears that threatened to fall, Aspen turned around, heading to her car.

"Go get Brianna. We leaving," Aspen called out to Justice.

Aspen couldn't take anymore. She refused to listen to Moe's lies. She also refused to stand there while Dominque threw the fact that she was carrying Moe's child in her face. She'd been able to hold in her tears long enough for her to get inside her car. However, as soon as she closed the door, Aspen broke down. Her feelings were crushed, and her heart was completely broken as she realized her entire relationship had been a lie.

"We need to be beating the dog shit outta both they asses!" Brianna yelled out, swinging Aspen's driver's side door open.

"Girl, get yo drunk ass in this car so that we can go," Justice ordered. She knew Aspen had had enough and wouldn't be able to take much more.

"Yeah, bitch, you betta listen to yo lil home girl before I have my people come out here and handle yo ass!" Dominque yelled.

Dominque didn't give a damn about being pregnant. There was no way she was going to allow any female to come to her party and try and punk her. She might not fight while she was pregnant, but she had three sisters inside the house that would fight for her, no questions asked.

"Handle me? Who gon' handle me?" Brianna replied, quoting Megan Thee Stallion.

With that, Justice opened the back passenger door and all but threw Brianna inside, closing the door behind her. Once they all were inside the car, Aspen pulled off, trying to get as far away from Moe as fast as possible.

"Aspen, are you okay, girl? That was some straight bull-shit. I can't believe that nigga did that shit. I'm sorry, but I was ready to beat the fuck outta them for you." Brianna spoke sympathetically.

"Yeah, Aspen, that shit ain't right at all. I ain't even know they knew each other," Justice added.

"I know y'all didn't know. Shit, neither did I. I ain't gonna lie. Shit hurt like a muthafucka. But I'ma be cool. Fuck him."

"It's cool. We 'bout to get drunk and burn all that nigga's shit in the backyard," Justice suggested.

"Bitch, we gonna do what?" Aspen questioned with a chuckle.

'Wait, nah, bitch, that sound like fun. That nigga got his shit at yo crib. Expensive shit at that. It's gonna hurt his ego and his pockets if we burn all that shit," Brianna uttered, liking Justice's idea.

"Y'all both crazy as hell. But let's do it," Aspen agreed.

They pulled into Aspen's driveway and went inside the house. Aspen went directly upstairs, gathering Moe's belongings. Brianna went into the kitchen. She cut up a few lemons and grabbed a bottle of tequila from the cabinet while Justice went out back and started a fire. Aspen threw a handful of Moe's belongings on the ground in front of the fire before running up to retrieve the last of his items.

"This all his stuff?" Justice asked, looking down at the small pile.

"Yeah, that's everything he had here," Aspen responded.

"Girl, burning this lil ass shit ain't gonna do nothing to him. In real life, he probably not even gonna come back for this shit. I thought he had more stuff here." Brianna spoke.

"So, now y'all don't want to burn his shit?" Aspen questioned.

"I mean, yeah, we can still burn it. But if you really wanna hit him where it hurts, then we need to do something else," Brianna informed, picking up a pair of Moe's jeans and throwing them into the fire.

"Bri is right, Aspen. We need to think of something else."

"Okay, then what's the something else, y'all?" Aspen asked, waiting on her friends to tell her their next move.

"Let's fuck his car up. That would really have him fucked up. Everybody that knows Moe knows how much he loves that Rover," Brianna suggested.

"Yeah, fuckin' with his car sounds good and all but he gonna know that's her. Fuckin' with his car just screams bitter ass ex. We need to think of something else." Justice spoke. She sat there in deep thought as she attempted to figure out a master plan. Within seconds, she looked up at Aspen with a huge smile on her face, as if a light bulb had just gone off in her head.

"I got it, bitch. We gonna rob him," Justice blurted out.

"Bitch, what? Okay, you cut off. Don't give this bitch no more to drink." Brianna laughed.

"Shut up. I ain't drunk, hoe. Just hear me out. We all know that nigga is a hustla and ain't nothing more important to a hustla than they money. If we take that shit, I bet that nigga feel that shit."

Aspen looked at Justice and saw she was serious. Aspen wanted to hurt Moe just as he'd hurt her. However, she didn't think they could get away with a robbery.

"What if he finds out it's us?" Aspen questioned.

"He won't. We gonna dress up as niggas and disguise our voices. He will never know it's us as long as we do it right."

"Wait, nah, I think Justice could be on to something. We could get some real baggy clothes and some Pooh Shiesty masks. That nigga ah just think some random ass niggas robbed him. Now, all we gotta do is find the right time and place to do it."

Now, it was Aspen's turn to think. She knew him the best out of the three, so she knew the places he would frequent. She thought about how Moe had just told her about a huge re-up he had coming up. She knew if they caught Moe at the right time, they might be able to get drugs and money.

"He got a re-up with Fabo on Friday. For this to work though, we gotta see him after his meeting with Fabo but before he gets back to his spot. Once he gets back to his spot, we gonna be outnumbered and outgunned." Aspen spoke.

Aspen knew from talking to Moe that he would be meeting with Fabo on Belle Isle at eight Friday night. So, if her girls were serious about robbing Moe, then they would be there too.

"Wait, bitch, you talkin' bout we gonna be outgunned if we wait for him to get back to his spot. But bitch, who the fuck has a gun in the first place? We don't even have one let alone three. So, how the fuck are we gonna rob Moe at a re-up spot where we know he gon' be strapped? If he thinks a random ass group of niggas is robbin' him, he gon' shoot," Brianna enlightened.

She wanted to get back at Moe for hurting Aspen just like the rest of them did, but she didn't want to die in the process. Brianna looked over at both Justice and Aspen as she waited for them to answer her.

"I can get some guns. That ain't no problem. Y'all know I stay in the hood. Now, as far as Moe goes, he would have to get to his gun first. With us having guns on him, he ain't gonna be able to do shit but what we say," Justice announced.

With that, their plan was in motion, and they'd just plotted their revenge on Moe. They were all happy with the outcome, and Aspen smiled for the first time since she'd caught Moe with Dominque. They spent the rest of the night taking a few tequila shots by the fire.

CHAPTER SEVEN

spen went to the mall and purchased everything they would need for their mission. She bought three pairs of black jeans, which she made sure were at least three sizes too big, three extra-large, long sleeved, black shirts, and three black ski masks. She even bought black gloves to cover their hands. Aspen was just about to walk out the mall when she remembered they would need shoes to wear. There was no way they would be able to rob Moe in shoes they already owned. Turning around, Aspen walked into Foot Locker and purchased three pairs of black Nikes.

Everything was set, and all Aspen had to do was wait for Justice and Brianna to get out of school and come to her house. Justice had let her know the night before that she'd purchased guns for the three of them with the money Aspen had given her. She also informed her that for another hundred, her cousin would let them use his car for the night. Aspen was nervous about the plan but wanted to get Moe back for hurting her even more.

Pulling back up to her house, she went inside and waited on Brianna and Justice to arrive. Her phone rung, and she knew it was one of them letting her know they were on the way. However, when she looked down at her phone and saw a number she didn't recognize, she hesitated to swipe the talk button. When her phone stopped ringing, she placed it back on her kitchen counter, going back into deep thought about the robbery she was about to commit. However, when the same number called right back, she decided to answer.

"Hello?'

"Damn, so you really not gonna talk to me anymore, huh?" A familiar voice spoke.

Aspen rolled her eyes, not ready for the bullshit she knew was about to take place. She hadn't spoken with Moe in an entire week and was not about to do so now. She knew that anything that came out his mouth would be a lie. She'd already told herself that she would never fuck with Moe ever again, and she was going to stand on that. There was nothing Moe could do or say to ever make Aspen be with him again, so his call was obsolete.

"Moe, I have nothing to say to you. After what you did, this what you call me and say? That alone lets me know yo ass is a narcissist, and I need to stay the fuck away from you."

Without another word, Aspen ended the call. The hurt

she'd once felt was gone and had been replaced by anger. "I just ain't gonna call him? How the fuck is I'm sorry not the first thing out his mouth? Man, fuck that nigga." Aspen spoke out loud. Any reservations she had about going through with their plan had just gone out the window. The way Moe thought that Aspen would just settle and still fuck with him after what he did to her had her heated.

Her doorbell rang, and she knew it was Brianna and Justice. She opened the door and allowed them inside, immediately informing them about Moe's call.

"That nigga ain't shit. That's why we 'bout to get his ass," Brianna stated.

"Hell yeah. I got all the stuff we gon' need too," Aspen informed.

They had about an hour and a half before the robbery was due to take place. So, they decided they would start getting ready. Each one of them brushed their hair into ponytails before placing wig caps over their heads. They dressed in their black baggy jeans and over-sized, long sleeve shirts before placing the ski masks over their heads.

"Bitch, you look like a nigga," Justice announced, looking over at Brianna.

"Bitch, so do you," Brianna replied.

"Yeah, this shit gonna work," Aspen spoke, disguising her voice to sound like a man.

"And bitch, you sound like one," they both laughed.

"Y'all ready for this shit? Cause it's about to go down," Aspen asked, placing the black gloves over her hands.

"I stay ready. Here you go," Justice answered, handing Aspen a pair of black sunglasses. "You can't rob nobody with them big ass gray eyes. He would know it's you off rip," she continued.

"Thank you," Aspen replied, taking the glasses. That had been the only thing she'd forgotten about. She was happy she had friends that had her back.

With that, the three of them walked out the house and into the dark green Buick Regal Justice borrowed from her cousin. They took the drive to Belle Isle, arriving on the island shortly after. They drove around for a couple of minutes before spotting Moe's Rover parked several feet away from the fountain.

"There he go right there." Aspen spotted.

Justice nodded, turning her headlights off before parking on the opposite side. They sat inside the car as they watched the fountain change from red to purple. A few moments later, they saw Fabo pull up and park next to Moe. With that, all three girls exited the car. Moe and Fabo were both too caught up in their business to notice the girls watching them from the other side of the fountain.

They watched as Fabo handed Moe a black duffle bag before saying a few words to him. They were too far away from the girls for them to know what he said, but they saw Moe nod his head. They shook hands before Fabo got back into his car while Moe went to put the duffle bag in his back-seat. The moment they saw Fabo pull off, Aspen, Brianna, and Justice sprang into action, pulling out their guns and running over to Moe.

"Run dat shit, nigga." Justice spoke in a deep baritone. She surprised herself, sounding more like a man than she thought she would. She held the gun to Moe's head as she watched him bitch up immediately.

"W-what you doin'? Say man, you ain't gotta rob me, man, please," Moe stuttered.

His entire body shook in fear as he felt the cold steel pressed against his head. He didn't want to die and prayed the gunman wouldn't pull the trigger. "Please don't do this shit to me, bro." He continued to beg.

Brianna walked in front of him, aiming her gun at him as well, and Moe knew there was no way out. "Run dem pockets, nigga." Brianna spoke. Moe emptied his pockets as he was told, giving his entire stack to Brianna.

"Them chains and them Buffs too, muthafucka."

As much as it broke his heart, Moe took off his chains and glasses and handed them to Brianna. His ego was shot to hell as he stood there being robbed for all his valuables. *Niggas in the hood gonna have a field day with this. I'ma be the punk of the city for gettin' my shit snatched.*

"Okay, y'all got all my shit. Please just leave. I ain't gon' say shit. I got a family I gotta live for. My girl is pregnant with our first child. I gotta get back to them," Moe pleaded.

Aspen was heated at the mention of Dominque and Moe having a family together. Grabbing the duffle bag out the backseat, she slammed the door. She walked over to Moe and stood next to Brianna.

"Nigga, don't nobody give a fuck 'bout you havin' no family," Aspen shot.

"Please not the bag. Y'all can take everything else, but that bag don't belong to me. If that shit comes up missin', so will I."

"Nigga, fuck you. We runnin' this shit." Aspen spoke before busting Moe in the head with the butt of her gun as hard as she could. When he fell to the ground, the three friends took off running toward the car.

"Man, we did that shit! Y'all see how that bitch ass nigga was stutterin' and shit?" Justice voiced as she drove off the island.

"Hell yeah, that shit was lit. Ain't no way he gonna even know that was us. We sounded so much like a group of niggas," Aspen agreed.

"I can't wait to see what we hit that nigga foe." Brianna spoke.

They were back in Aspen's neighborhood within twenty minutes. They parked the car up the street, just in case Moe just so happened to have spotted the car they got inside after the robbery; before they walked back to Aspen's house. They took off their disguises and changed back into their street clothes before counting their profits. They had six thousand in cash that they split between the three of them. They had also decided they would pawn the jewelry and glasses. When they opened the duffle bag and saw the kilos of cocaine inside, their eyes widened.

"This gotta be worth a lot of money," Brianna suggested.

Aspen pulled each brick out one by one until there was a total of six in front of them. They knew the weight could get them money, but none of them knew exactly how much. The three friends were as green to the drug game as three toddlers, having no clue how to sell cocaine.

"How the hell we gonna get this shit off?" Aspen asked out loud. It was clear to all three of them that they had not thought their plan all the way through. There was no way Aspen could have six bricks of cocaine just sitting inside her house with no way to sell them.

"I can call Trae. He'll know what to do with them," Justice suggested, grabbing her phone to call her cousin.

"Wait!" Brianna yelled out, grabbing Justice's phone from her hand.

"Bitch, what the fuck is wrong with you? Why you grabbin' my shit like that?" Justice questioned.

"We can't call just anybody and tell them we got six kilos. First off, they gonna wonder how we got them. Second, if word not out yet 'bout Moe being robbed, it will be by tomorrow. We don't want nobody to know we had anything to do with that shit," Brianna enlightened.

Aspen nodded her head in agreement. Brianna was right, and they all knew it.

"We need to call somebody that we can trust completely," Brianna continued.

"Well, shit, I don't have nobody to call because everyone I trust is sitting in this room," Aspen stated.

Brianna and Justice both thought for several seconds before Brianna spoke again. "Why don't we call Ant but just tell him we have one or two?"

"Now that might work. Call him," Aspen replied.

Ant was Brianna's uncle on her father's side. He was the only person any of them could think of that really knew the drug game. Aspen knew Ant had done business with her father and uncle back in the day and had never heard them speak anything but highly of him. So, she was comfortable with Brianna's suggestion.

"Make the call," Aspen announced.

Brianna picked up her phone, placing the call to her uncle, not giving him much detail. She told him she came across a brick and needed his help. Brianna gave Ant her location and waited on him to arrive. Ant knocked on the door fifteen minutes later, ready to help his niece.

"Where y'all get it from?" Ant asked.

"My dude just got locked up, and he left it for me to sell," Justice lied.

Ant nodded his head while he examined the kilo. "You owe somebody for this package?" Ant asked.

"Nah, the money gonna be for me to hold me over til he gets out," Justice replied.

"I'll give you sixteen for it right now. You don't need to be walkin' round here with this shit on you."

"Sixteen what?" Aspen asked.

"Sixteen thousand. This a kilo, and I ain't gonna lie. You could get a few thousand more if you sold it on the street. But I can buy it right now. And since you won't owe nobody for this package, it's gonna be profit right in yo hand. That few thousand ain't really no loss." Ant spoke.

Justice looked over at Aspen. When Justice saw her nod her head, she agreed to sell the product. "It was nice doing business with y'all. Let me know if y'all come across anymore of this shit to sell." Ant spoke before walking out the door.

"Bitch, sixteen fuckin' racks? I ain't never held this much money in my hands," Justice yelled excitedly.

"And we still got five more left to sell. We 'bout to have some money for real, y'all," Brianna chimed in.

They sat at Aspen's kitchen table, laughing about the events that took place that night, as they counted their money. Seeing how it was both Brianna and Justice's senior year of high school, they made plans to have the best prom sendoff and graduation party money could buy, while Aspen planned to put half of her money away, starting a stash for Cove for when she came home. Her sister had made sure she was okay while she was in prison, so Aspen would damn sure make sure she was straight when she got out.

. . .

IN TWO WEEKS, Ant had come and picked up three more kilos from the girls. The stuff they had was the best product he'd had in a long time, and it was moving fast. It was almost out yet again, so he hit Brianna up for another package.

"Okay, I got you. I get out of school at three, so I'll meet you at Aspen's house after that."

"Cool," Ant replied before ending the call.

Brianna couldn't believe how fast they were making money with Ant. At only seventeen, she was sitting on twenty-five thousand dollars and couldn't help but to feel like "that girl." She walked out the school building and made her way to her mother's car.

"Hey, Ma."

"Hey, baby. How was your day at school?" Shanté asked.

"It was cool. Can you drop me off at Aspen's house?"

"Yeah, I'll drop you off. I wanna see how she doin' anyway," Shanté replied.

When they arrived at Aspen's house, Brianna shot a text to her, letting her know Shanté was coming inside. Aspen opened the door with a huge smile on her face and allowed them both into the house. She greeted Shanté with a loving hug. Aspen loved Shanté. She'd been the closest thing she had to a mother since her mother passed away, so she would always be welcomed in Aspen's home.

"I'm glad to see you, Shanté," Aspen cooed.

"Me too. I haven't seen you in weeks, but I can see you're doing well. I wanted you to know that I'm going to see your sister tomorrow. I know she said she didn't want you to see her in prison, but it's been two years, so maybe she's changed her mind. If you want, I can ask her if she would let me bring you with me next time."

Aspen's eyes lit up at the mention of seeing her sister. She wanted nothing more than to see Cove. She was the only family Aspen had left, and she missed her tremendously. If Shanté could talk Cove into letting Aspen come see her, Aspen would be there with bells on.

"Okay, I'ma talk to her, and I'll let you know what she says. I'm about to head out and let you two have y'all girl time." Shanté spoke before walking out the door.

"Damn, bitch, I thought she would never leave. Ant is on his way over to re-up," Brianna informed.

"Damn, he going through that shit fast as hell. I don't know what he gonna do when we run out. That nigga gonna be mad as hell," Aspen stated.

Several moments later, Ant was knocking at Aspen's door. "What up doe?" Ant greeted, walking inside Aspen's house.

"Hey, Ant, we only got two bricks left then that's it. Ain't gonna be no more coming from us," Aspen informed.

"Damn, what? I was getting comfortable getting my work from y'all. I guess I'ma just take both of them now and make it easier."

"Cool with me. Lemme go grab 'em." Aspen spoke before walking out the room.

When she returned, she handed the two bricks to Ant, informing him that she would give them both to him for thirty instead of the sixteen apiece he usually paid. She felt as though he deserved a discount for taking all the kilos off their hands as quickly as he'd done. Ant agreed and handed Aspen the money.

"If y'all come across some more, let me know. Y'all always gonna have a customer in me."

"Fasho. If we get anything else, you gonna be the first to know," Brianna replied.

Ant walked out the door, and Aspen and Brianna sat at the table and split the money they'd just made three ways. Aspen placed a call to Justice and let her know she was on her way to pick her up. She couldn't wait to tell her about the money they'd just gotten and didn't want to do so over the phone. When they pulled up to Justice's apartment, they walked inside without knocking.

"What up doe?" Justice greeted.

"We are like all the way up," Brianna responded.

"Huh?" Justice questioned, confused about Brianna's response.

"You heard her. We all the way up. We just made thirty racks off Ant. He bought the last two bricks we had," Aspen announced.

"Damn, we really ain't got no more shit left, huh?" Justice asked.

She'd been getting comfortable making the money they'd been making. She was getting used to the money coming so fast and didn't want it to stop. Justice had been spending money left and right and wasn't saving as much money as Brianna and Aspen were. The portion of the thirty thousand they'd just made was all she had. Justice wanted more. Hell, she needed more. Justice had grown up in the projects with nothing. Her mother tried her best to provide; however, it just wasn't enough. She was tired of being poor and knew she wasn't going to continue to be that way.

"Nope, we all out. Ant took everything we had," Aspen confirmed.

"We gon' have to get some more. We can't just up and stop now. We need money coming in at all times." Justice spoke.

"Bitch, we already got money. What you mean?" Brianna questioned. She was comfortable with the money she'd made from the robbery. In days, Brianna had gone from having no money to more money than she'd had in her entire life. So, she didn't understand why Justice was tripping.

"That money ain't gonna last forever, Bri. This shit barely enough to last us a couple months. Shit, after prom, I'ma be broke. I ain't even gonna have enough for no damn graduation party."

"So, what you wanna do, Justice?" Aspen asked.

"Shit, I wanna get at some more dope boys," Justice answered.

"Bitch, what? That shit was a one-time thing. We ain't no fuckin' thieves. We only did that shit cause of what Moe did to Aspen. Now yo ass wanna just go out and rob random ass D boys? Fuck is wrong with you? Did you smoke some of that work we took?" Brianna yelled out in evident disagreement.

Aspen, however, thought about what Justice said and agreed with her. The money they had now wouldn't last forever. She had bills to pay, and she also wanted to save more money for Cove.

"When you wanna do it, and who you wanna get?" Aspen asked.

"Aspen, you can't be serious. Are you really gonna agree with her?" Brianna asked in disbelief.

"What we gonna do when the money runs out? Get a job? You want us to go from making thousands of dollars in five minutes to makin' eight dollars an hour? I can't do no nine to five," Aspen asked.

Although Brianna didn't want to rob anyone else, she knew they were both right. As much money as she had, she also had things to spend it on. Brianna saw how fast the money came after the robbery, and she knew that if she got a real job, she would never have that type of money. At seventeen, she could only get a job at some greasy fast-food place, and that was definitely not her thing. So, with that, she did the only thing she thought she could. She agreed.

"I say we get at Mookie," Justice suggested.

"Mookie? Since when that nigga start getting money?" Brianna questioned.

Mookie was a young hustler that lived in Justice's neighborhood. They didn't really know him but had seen him around for years. Justice had been noticing he'd been getting his weight up for a minute now, and Justice was ready to take it.

"That nigga must be working for somebody cause that nigga really out here getting money. I saw that shit. He getting money, and we gon' take it," Justice informed, wanting to let her girls know this was, indeed, a good move. "He always posted at Fast Franks. I know we can catch his ass there," she continued.

"When y'all tryin' to do this?" Aspen asked, clearly down for whatever.

"Shit, tomorrow. We already got everything we need, so why wait? Let's get this shit done," Justice replied.

They all agreed, and Aspen and Brianna left. Aspen dropped Brianna off at her house before driving back home. When she got there, she went up to her bathroom immediately and ran herself a bubble bath. As she sat in the hot water, she thought about the robbery she was about to commit. When they robbed Moe, it was only for revenge. Aspen had no idea they would make as much money as they did. However, now they were about to make this a lifestyle. Aspen had made thousands of dollars in five minutes, so she knew the business would be lucrative. She became excited about her new business venture and all the money she was sure to make.

THE NEXT DAY, both Brianna and Justice arrived at Aspen's house early that afternoon. Brianna's mind had changed overnight, and they were all excited about the hit as they anticipated the money they were about to make. Justice was able to borrow another one of her cousin's cars, and they used the disguises and guns from their hit on Moe, so everything was set. They knew that Mookie would be at Fast Franks, serving his customers, and planned to ambush him and take everything he had. They knew this would be easy money, and they were ready to get it.

Right before they were ready to walk out the door, Aspen's phone rang. Looking down at it, she saw it was Shanté and answered it. "Hey, Ms. Shanté. What's up?"

"Hey, Aspen. I was just calling to let you know I went and saw Cove. She's okay, holding her own in there. I'm sorry, baby. She doesn't want you to come see her yet. She says she don't want you to see her like that. But I'm sure she will change her mind. I told her how much you miss her and want to see her. I'ma keep talking to her. I'm sure she will come around at some point."

"Thanks for tryin', Ms. Shanté. We write each other a lot, so I knew she didn't want me to visit her in prison. I just thought it might be different if it came from you," Aspen replied.

"I'm sorry, Aspen, but I'ma keep talkin' to her about it. I promise."

Aspen ended the call, and the three friends took the twenty-minute drive out to Inkster. As Justice got off 94 at the Inkster Road exit, she drove down the street toward Fast Franks.

"That's that nigga right there, sittin' in his car," Justice announced as she passed by the liquor store.

She made a U-turn as she turned back around and turned onto New York Street. She parked the car, and the three of them got out, running through the back entrance of the parking lot. They ran up to Mookie's car, catching him off guard.

"Run dat shit." Aspen spoke in a deep baritone.

"What? Nigga, get the fuck outta here with dat shit," Mookie responded, feeling untouchable.

"Nah, nigga, you get the fuck outta here with that shit," Justice uttered, placing her gun through the passenger window, and aiming it at Mookie's head.

"Oh, bro got that dawg shit on em. Say less. Y'all got it." Mookie surrendered.

Brianna looked around, making sure Mookie was at the store alone, while Aspen put everything Mookie had in her pockets. As fast as they ran up on Mookie, they ran away and back to their car. They drove off quickly, heading back to 94.

"Damn, that shit was a rush," Brianna announced.

"Hell yeah, it was. I can't wait to see what we made this time." Justice spoke.

They made their way back to Aspen's house. When they walked inside, they immediately went to her kitchen table to count their earnings. Aspen emptied her pockets, and they began counting.

"I know you fuckin' lyin'. This can't be all we made." Justice scoffed.

"Bitch, I told yo ass that nigga wasn't getting no money! Listenin' to yo ass and now this shit was a bust," Brianna yelled.

Aspen couldn't do anything but shake her head as she looked at the array of fives and tens mixed in with a few twenties and fifties. Once it was all counted, they realized they only had a thousand dollars and a fake Rolex. The shit was still ticking as Aspen held it in her hands.

"Justice, what made you think that nigga was getting money out here?" Aspen asked.

"Cause he is. I told you I saw it. We just hit him at the wrong time. We need to hit his ass again," Justice replied.

"Oh, hell nah. We ain't never double dippin'. We hit a nigga one time and one time only. Now, I'm down to hit another lick but never the same nigga twice," Brianna stated.

"Yeah, I'm with Bri on that shit. It's one and done," Aspen reiterated.

"Fine, so who we getting at next? Whoever it is, we need

to make sure we hit them at the right time because this was pointless." Justice spoke.

"Well, you picked him. I neva wanted to hit him in the first place. I knew that nigga was broke," Brianna replied.

"What about Surpo? But not just him, we need to hit his spot," Justice suggested.

"At his spot? Bitch, are you crazy? You tryin' to go to jail for breakin' and enterin'? Or you tryin' to get shot by one of the goons that be at the spot?" Brianna enlightened.

"Jail? Fuck outta here. What Bun B say? Muthafuck the judge, prosecutor, and the DA. Besides, what they gon' call and say? Somebody robbed my drug house? Girl, we ain't goin' to no damn jail off this shit. And we ain't getting shot either. Are you forgettin' we got guns too?" Justice spoke, showing her hunger to get money. She didn't care how many dope boys she had to rob to become rich. She would take them all.

"Actually, I don't think that's a bad idea. We all know Surpo for sure gettin' that bread, and if we rob his spot, we will get everything he got, instead of just the little shit he may have on him. I ain't tryna do this shit forever, and I know y'all ain't either. But in order for us to stack some real money, we gonna need some real paydays. Takin' Surpo's spot would be just that." Aspen agreed.

Brianna thought for several moments before she spoke again. "If we gon' start takin' nigga's spots, then we gonna have to have an airtight plan. I don't want none of us getting hurt, so we can't be sloppy with this shit."

They all agreed, deciding they would plan their mission out completely and set it for the following Saturday. They were all excited because they knew hitting Surpo's spot would deem to be extremely lucrative. Soon, they would be calling Ant, letting him know they were back on.

CHAPTER EIGHT

The day of the robbery came quickly. They decided they would run in on Surpo at ten-thirty in the morning, wanting to assure they got them at the best time. They had even put their money together and bought a car to commit their robberies in. They didn't want to continue using other peoples' cars out of fear it would lead right back to them. So, they cut out the middleman and bought their own ride strictly for the robberies.

The three girls, dressed in their same disguises, made their way to their Jeep, and headed to the east side. They pulled up to Surpo's spot and parked two houses down, casing the house for several moments.

"Y'all ready?" Aspen asked.

"We stay ready," Justice and Brianna replied in unison.

They got out the car and ran up to the stash house. Justice

knocked on the door, and as soon as it opened, the three girls rushed inside, catching the man that opened the door off guard.

"Where the shit at, nigga?" Brianna asked in her disguised tone as she pointed her gun directly at the man's head. She recognized the man as Vudoe, Surpo's young goon.

"I don't know what the fuck you talkin' 'bout." Vudoe stood his ground.

"Dawg, you think we playin' with you? I'll body yo ass right here and find that shit myself," Justice chimed in. showing Vudoe they were there to stand on business.

Knowing the robbers were serious, and not wanting to die, he told them were everything was. Vudoe was the only person in the house, so he knew he was outnumbered. At only eighteen years old, he wasn't ready to die. So, he would give them any information they needed in order to save his life at that moment, not giving a damn about the repercussions it might have on him later on.

Justice and Aspen ran to the back, while Brianna continued to hold Vudoe at gun point. They filled their duffle bags with all the weight and money that was inside the room, not leaving anything behind. Within minutes, they were out the house and back in their Jeep, peeling off down the street.

"Bitch, that shit was easy as fuck. Vudoe lil young ass was the only one there." Brianna beamed, feeling a rush of adrenaline from the robbery.

"Hell yeah. I bet they wish they wouldn't have left him

there alone. We took everything they had out that bitch. They gon' come back there to nothin'. I can't wait to see how much we took dem fo'." Aspen spoke.

They arrived at Aspen's house, and she parked the Jeep in her garage before they went into the house. They went to the kitchen table and began emptying the duffle bags. Justice began counting the weight, while Aspen and Brianna counted the money. When they were done, they realized they had twenty thousand in cash and ten kilos of cocaine. Robbing Surpo's spot had indeed been a huge payday, making all three of them happy. Brianna placed a call to Ant immediately, informing him they were back on. That was the best news Ant had heard all day, and he told Brianna he would be there in a couple of hours to re-up.

Over the next month, the girls had robbed another local dope spot, which made them ten thousand dollars and four more kilos. They were living their best lives without a care in the world. There was a month before prom, and Aspen, Brianna, and Justice walked through Sommerset, looking for prom dresses. Although Aspen had dropped out of school, she was still going to the prom as Justice's plus one. All three of them would be slaying prom, and Aspen couldn't wait for the after party they had planned.

"Bitch, this shit bout to be lit. I rented a Maybach and a driver to take us to prom and everything. We bout to have the best prom ever," Justice informed.

"Hell yeah, we are. These bitches bout to gag once they see us." Brianna agreed.

Once they all found the perfect dress, they decided to go to Jay Alexander for lunch. They ate good and spoke about the things they wanted to do with the money they were making. They planned to do another robbery. Not only did they have prom and graduation coming up, all three of their birthdays were right around the corner. Brianna's was the first coming up in June. She planned a party at Belle Isle and was inviting everyone to come through.

She knew that both her girls would still be underage, and she didn't want to do too much if her girls couldn't attend. Having a party on the Island would allow everyone to have fun. She was going to go all out for her Hawaiian themed party.

They planned to hit Grill right before prom, and Brianna was down for it. She knew that hitting Grill would give her money for her birthday party and money to stack as well. Grill was a hustler out of Southwest Detroit and was moving major weight in the city. This would be a bigger hit than the one on Surpo, and they all knew it.

It was the day before prom, and while all the other girls their age were getting their hair and nails done, the three of them were preparing to commit a robbery. They dressed in their all-black, street nigga attire and walked out the door, heading to Southwest Detroit. They'd hit Surpo's spot in the morning and found it was easy. So, they kept the exact same routine with this robbery.

Brianna pulled up down the street, and they watched the house for several moments. They didn't see any movement in the home, and there were no cars parked outside. The girls were skeptical about anyone being inside the house at all. They were just about to get out their Jeep when they saw a car pull up. They watched as a man got out the car holding a bag of white takeout containers. They watched in silence as he walked onto the porch and inside the house.

"Okay, we know for sure there's at least one dude in there." Brianna observed. "Y'all ready?" she continued.

"We stay ready," Aspen and Justice replied in unison.

Getting out the Jeep, they ran up on the porch, and Brianna knocked on the door. The same man they'd just seen enter the house was the one to open the door, and Brianna hoped that meant he was there alone.

"Yo, we not open yet. Come back at one," the man stated as if the trap house had office hours.

He tried to close the door, but Brianna placed her foot inside it, stopping it from closing. Before he could say anything, Justice and Aspen burst through the door, guns aimed.

"Y'all muthafuckas got a death wish or somethin'? Cause that's exactly what's gonna happen, comin' here with that shit," the goon spoke.

"Shut the fuck up and run dat shit," Brianna interrupted.

"I ain't givin y'all shit. Y'all gon' have to kill me."

"Nigga, don't tempt me," Justice spoke, walking up to the goon and placing her gun to his temple.

"Alright, alright," the goon surrendered quickly. "It's in the kitchen, but y'all ain't gon' get away with it, so y'all might as well leave it there."

With that, Brianna walked toward the kitchen with Aspen following. They quickly began grabbing everything they saw, filling both their duffle bags. Brianna smiled at the amount of work and money they were getting. Both of their duffle bags were full, and there was still money on the table. Knowing they weren't going to leave anything behind, she ran to get the bag Justice had. She was just about to ask Justice for her bag when she saw a man walking through the door, holding a gun.

In that split second, she knew it was either her cousin's life or the goon's life. It was a no brainer. Brianna raised her gun and fired two shots. One hit the goon in the neck and sent him falling to the floor.

Justice jumped in fear when she heard the shots and turned around quickly to see what was happening. In the half second it took for her to turn her head, the other goon grabbed Justice's gun. He took it out her hand and aimed at her in one swift motion. Justice knew she'd fucked up by taking her eyes off the man she was robbing. Now, she was about to pay for that mistake with her life. She heard the loud gunshot and saw the goon fall to the floor. She smiled in relief when she saw Aspen behind her holding her smoking gun.

"We gotta get the fuck outta here," Brianna yelled frantically as she looked down at the two dead men laying across the floor. Aspen ran to the back of the house and grabbed the two duffle bags before running back to the front. She handed one to Justice, and they all left the house, jumping into their Jeep and pulling off down the street.

"Bitch, we just fuckin' killed two people. What the fuck are we gonna do? We was only supposed to be robbin' niggas, not killin' them. I ain't sign up for this shit," Brianna cried.

She was terrified and didn't want to go to prison for murder. She was so nervous that she couldn't stop shaking as she drove as fast as she could toward the freeway. She prayed that no one heard the shots or saw them leaving the house.

"Calm down, Bri. Everything gonna be okay." Justice tried to reason.

"Bitch, how? We just killed two people. We going to jail," Brianna continued.

"Jail? Bitch, that's the last thing you need to be worried about. If anybody did see us, they definitely ain't gonna be tellin' the police. If they tell anyone, they would tell Grill. That's who we need to be worried 'bout," Justice informed.

"Oh, my God, we gonna die!" Brianna cried even harder. She swerved and almost hit a parked car as tears clouded her vision.

"Bitch, calm the fuck down and drive this car right before

you kill us trying to get away from a murder. If anybody did see us, they lookin' for three men, not three women. All we gotta do is get rid of this car, and we good," Aspen stated.

Brianna knew Aspen was right, so, with that, she was able to calm down enough to drive. She was still shaken up by the fact they'd just taken two lives. However, knowing no one was looking for them specifically put her mind at ease. She parked the car in Aspen's garage, and the three of them exited, walking into the house. Aspen immediately went to the kitchen and grabbed a black trash bag.

"Take them clothes off and put them in here. We gonna burn them tonight," she ordered as she began taking off her clothes. Brianna and Justice follow suit, removing their clothes and placing them inside the trash bag.

"What we gonna do with the car?" Brianna asked.

"We gonna take it somewhere and burn that bitch too," Justice informed.

"Hell yeah, we gonna take it to Ohio and burn it. We can do that shit tonight," Aspen stated.

"They ain't gonna be able to trace that truck to us. We never got that shit registered. Them fake ass thirty-day tags we kept puttin' on that shit ain't got no real name on it. We gonna be good," she continued.

That night, that was exactly what they did. Aspen got in her G-Wagon and followed Justice and Brianna as they made their way to Ohio. Justice's heart beat fast as she drove, praying they didn't get pulled over by the police. Once they crossed the Ohio state limits, they found a field right off the freeway. There didn't look to be anyone around for miles, and they figured it would be a good place to dump the car. Since there was no way for the car to be traced back to them, they decided not to burn it and just leave it in the field instead.

When they got back to Aspen's house, they burned the clothes in the backyard as planned. All three girls were still on edge but were becoming calmer by the minute. They had enough money and weight to hold them over. So, they decided they would wait until things died down before going on another mission.

CHAPTER NINE

It was the day of prom, and they all met at Brianna's house for their prom send off. No one would have ever guessed they'd just murdered two people just twenty-four hours earlier. All of Justice and Brianna's family was there to see them off. However, to Aspen, it was bittersweet. She didn't have any family there to take pictures with or to tell her how beautiful she looked in her dress. Any family she had was either dead or in jail, and it was times like this that she wished her life had turned out differently. She wore a long, pink gown with hundreds of hand placed Swarovski crystals all over it. She had everything professionally done from her makeup to her nails and everything in between, including her hair and lashes.

Shanté could see that Aspen's spirits were down, and she already knew the reason. So, she tried her best to lift her up.

She knew she wasn't her mother, but she loved Aspen like her own daughter and would do anything to put a smile on her face.

"Come on, pretty in pink, let's take some pictures," Shanté offered. Smiling, Aspen posed for several pictures with Shanté.

Brianna stood at the other end of the lawn, taking pictures with her uncle. She wore a long, red dress which fit tightly on her body, hugging every one of her curves. It had a long split down the side which stopped about two inches before her hips. Her hair was in a half up half down style, and her makeup was flawless.

Justice stood next to her wearing a yellow dress with gold accessories. All three of the girls looked equally beautiful. They posed for pictures together before getting into their Maybach and heading to prom.

Their prom was beautiful, decorated in a Paris theme. The girls had the time of their lives as they partied the night away. Aspen socialized and took pictures with classmates she hadn't seen since she left the school. It was indeed a night to remember.

"Bitch, why the fuck is Moe here?" Justice announced as she spotted him walking through the door. Both Brianna and Aspen looked over to see Moe walking toward them.

"I knew I would be able to find you here. You look so beautiful." He spoke.

"She knows she looks good, and she don't want to talk to

yo ass. You don't even go to this school. How the fuck did you get in here?" Justice stated.

"I believe I was talkin' to Aspen, not you," he shot back.

"Moe, I don't have shit to say to you. You look like a fool even coming up here. I already told you we was done, so you coming up here was stupid."

Moe looked into Aspen's eyes, her beautiful gray eyes that he hadn't stared into for months. He missed her so much. He knew he'd done her wrong; he just wished she would talk to him, so he could apologize the way he wanted to. He knew she was hurt, and he couldn't blame her for not talking to him. However, he'd hoped things would be different face to face. He'd hoped that once she saw him, all the feelings she had for him would come back. However, as she stood in front of him at that moment, that wasn't the case.

"I just wanted to tell you I was sorry for everything I put you through. Even if you never speak to me again, at least I can say I was able to apologize," he informed.

"Apology not accepted. You can leave now," Aspen stated before walking off. She wasn't about to stand there and listen to anymore of his lies. She was having a great time at prom and wouldn't allow Moe to ruin that for her.

"Girl, fuck him. He ain't shit anyway." Justice spoke.

"Bitch, I already know. I ain't thinkin' 'bout his ass. He ruined what we had, not me. I don't feel bad at all," Aspen responded.

. . .

AFTER PROM, they all headed to Aspen's house where the after party would take place. Her house was packed from wall to wall with half the senior class. There was liquor flowing and blunts in rotation as the music played. They partied well into the early morning hours. The sun was on its way up once the partygoers began to leave. They had so much fun. They'd even forgotten they'd just murdered two people.

"Bitch, I'm drunk as hell," Brianna informed, plopping down on the couch.

"Shit, me too. I'm 'bout to go get under the bed. I'll see y'all when I wake up," Aspen informed, walking drunkenly up the stairs, heading to her room.

The three friends slept all day, not walking up until around six that evening. They were all starving when they woke up, so Aspen decided to call in an order at the soul food spot around the corner. She left to go pick the food up, leaving Brianna and Justice at her house. Brianna sat on the couch, scrolling through Netflix, trying to find a movie to watch while they ate. There was a knock at the door, and at first, Brianna wasn't going to answer it. She knew it wasn't Aspen because Aspen had a key to her own house. However, after several moments of the person knocking on the door, she decided to see who it was.

"Who the hell knocking on the door like that?" Justice asked, running down the stairs.

"I don't know. I'm about to look now." Brianna spoke,

walking up to the door and looking out the peephole. "It's Moe," Brianna whispered.

"Fuck do he want? Didn't Aspen tell him she don't wanna speak to him anymore? Why can't that nigga listen?"

Justice walked to the door, moving Brianna out the way, so she could open it. However, when Brianna noticed what she was about to do, she quickly attempted to stop her. "Don't open it. You know damn well Aspen don't want him in here."

"Relax. I ain't lettin' that nigga in here. I'm just gonna tell his ass to get away from the door. He already showed up to prom. I'm starting to think he stalkin' her. I don't want Aspen to come home and see him here," Justice replied.

Brianna nodded her head okay and watched as Justice opened the door. "Why the fuck are you here? Didn't Aspen tell you she…"

Whack!

Before Justice could even finish her sentence, Moe had bust her in the face so hard that it sent her crashing to the floor. He walked into the home, and Brianna screamed as she attempted to run. However, she was halted when Moe grabbed a handful of her hair.

"Where the fuck is Aspen?" he yelled.

"She not here," Brianna yelled back.

"Then we gon' wait for her to come back," he responded before slamming her head into the wall, knocking her out instantly.

. . .

ASPEN PAID for their order and grabbed the food before heading back to her car. Her stomach was growling from being empty the entire day. She couldn't wait to eat. All she wanted to do was relax on her couch with a plate of food, a movie, and her girls. She'd consumed a lot of liquor the night before, and it had her feeling sluggish.

When she arrived home, Aspen parked her truck in her driveway, grabbed the food, and walked into the house. "I hope y'all bitches found somethin' for us to watch. This food smellin' good, and I'm ready to eat," Aspen called out.

Walking farther into her home, she was stunned to see both Brianna and Justice tied to her dining room chairs. "What the fuck?" Aspen immediately rushed over to her two friends, attempting to untie Brianna first. However, before she could loosen the tight knots any further, Moe came out of nowhere, startling her, causing her to fall back.

"Moe, what the fuck are you doing here? Did you do this to them? Get yo crazy ass the fuck out my house right now. Fuck is wrong with you?" Aspen stood to her feet and continued to attempt to untie Brianna.

Moe didn't speak. Instead, he pulled his gun from his waistline and aimed it at Aspen, causing her to jump back again. She didn't know why Moe was in her house. She'd told him the day before that she didn't want to speak with him anymore, and she thought he would just move on. Now here he was, standing in her dining room, aiming a gun at her with her two friends tied up.

"Please, Moe, put the gun down. You don't have to do this," Aspen pleaded.

Moe walked closer to Aspen as she took steps backward, trying to keep space between them. She knew she would have to untie her friends for them to have any chance of survival. However, she didn't see any other way to do so without being shot first.

"Moe, please let us go. This is crazy. All this because you cheated on Aspen and now she don't want to be with you? Doing shit like this ain't gonna make her wanna be with you. If anything, she definitely ain't gonna fuck with you after this." Justice spoke.

Moe looked over at Justice and laughed sinisterly. She looked into his eyes and saw something that put fear in her heart, so she decided to stop talking.

"When I came to y'all prom yesterday, I had really came to apologize. I know I did you wrong, and that's something I didn't want to do. I loved you, Aspen, whether you believe it or not," he spoke.

Moe looked deep into Aspen's eyes before he continued. "I swallowed my pride and tried to apologize to you face to face like a fuckin' man. You didn't want to hear that shit. And I get it cause I fucked up. But when the three of y'all walked away, I noticed something I didn't see before."

"What the fuck are you talkin' 'bout, Moe?" Aspen asked, perplexed.

"Y'all bitches robbed me," Moe revealed.

Aspen's eyes widened at Moe's revelation. She had no idea Moe would ever figure out it was them. She'd thought they'd hidden their identity enough; however, now she knew that wasn't the case. Brianna, who was still trying to untie herself, watched Moe's every move. She observed his body language, and she knew this was not going to end well. She needed to untie herself and help her friend before it was too late.

"Moe, cut the bullshit. You know we ain't rob you. Is this yo way of tryna get me to talk to you again? Doing this shit ain't gonna make me wanna talk to you," Aspen stated.

Moe was infuriated at the fact that Aspen was trying to insult his intelligence. When the robbery first occurred, he'd indeed thought it was three men. He had no idea who even knew he would be on the Island at that time to re-up. It took him a long time to even remember he'd told Aspen about it. Even after remembering he'd told her, he still didn't realize it was them. It wasn't until he saw the three of them at prom that he'd put two and two together.

"You think cause you dress up like a nigga and change yo voice that I wouldn't recognize you? I know that body inside and out. I was the first nigga to ever know that body, and you thought you could pull one over on me?" Moe walked closer to Aspen, closing the gap between them. He wrapped one hand around her neck to let her know he wasn't playing games. "Bitch, I know it was y'all. Lyin' ain't gonna do shit but piss me off. You lucky I was able to pay Fabo back, but now, you gon' pay me back. You almost got away with the shit too until I saw the three of y'all together yesterday. That's when that shit clicked," he informed.

Still holding Aspen by the neck with one hand, he used his free hand to pull his penis from his sweatpants. He placed his hand inside her pants and began rubbing her treasure in an attempt to make it wet before putting his hand up to his nose and sniffing loudly. "Yeah, I missed this sweet shit. You 'bout to use nature's credit card to pay me back in installments starting now."

Aspen tried to wiggle her way out of his grasp once the reference of rape was mentioned. However, he was holding her too tightly for her to move even an inch. "Please don't do this," Aspen whispered.

"Bitch, shut the fuck up. Any sympathy I had for you went out the window the moment I realized you robbed me."

With that, he threw Aspen to the floor and got on top of her as tears streamed down her face. "If you move, I'ma blow yo fuckin' brains out yo head." Aspen knew he was telling the truth, so she was too afraid to move an inch. "I been missin' this shit," Moe whispered as he rubbed the tip of his hard dick over her yoni. Aspen shuddered in fear, knowing she was about to be violated. She couldn't do anything but cry as she laid there, awaiting her fate. She felt him enter her, but before he could even start moving, she heard a loud noise and felt Moe fall on top of her. She quickly crawled from under him as she watched Brianna hit him in the head repeatedly with the hammer.

"Bitch, I think he's dead," Aspen assumed as she watched the blood pour from his head.

Aspen rushed over to Justice and untied her before they both ran back over to where Brianna stood. "Give me the hammer, Bri," Aspen ordered.

Brianna stood there, shaking in fear, as she looked down at Moe's lifeless body. Just like that, the girls had caught their third body in under a week. The three of them stood there, not knowing what to do.

"We gotta get rid of this body," Justice informed.

"How, bitch? Where the fuck would we even take it?" Brianna asked.

"I don't know, but we gotta get him the fuck outta here," Aspen reiterated.

"Call Ant," Justice suggested, looking over at Brianna.

"Wait, do you really want to involve anyone else in this? I ain't trying to be caught up with no damn body," Aspen enlightened.

She was terrified. She knew that Brianna had killed Moe in self-defense. However, that didn't take away from the fact that he was lying dead in her dining room. She knew if Ant snitched, she would be the one going to prison.

"Ant is my uncle; he would never snitch, not on me. We can trust him for sure," Brianna assured.

Aspen thought for a moment. She remembered the bond

she shared with her own uncle when he was alive. *If their bond is anything like mine and my Uncle Donté then it's no way he's gonna snitch.* With that, Aspen told Brianna to make the call.

"DAMN, what the fuck happened here? When you called me and said you needed me, I damn sure didn't think it would be a dead body here," Ant spoke as he walked into Aspen's dining room.

There was so much blood all around the room. So, he knew they would have to do some extensive cleaning in order to remove it all. He was definitely going to help his niece by disposing of the body. However, he still wanted to know what happened and who the dead man was.

"That nigga came in here, tied me and Justice up, and tried to rape Aspen. So, when I got free, I hit his ass in the head with that damn hammer," Brianna recounted, pointing over at the bloody hammer.

"I'm glad you killed that nigga. Coming up in here, doing some weak ass shit like that," Ant informed.

"Aspen, do you have a large suitcase, something big enough to put this nigga in?" Ant asked.

Aspen thought for a moment before running upstairs and looking inside one of the guest room closets. She remembered Cove had several suitcases of all different sizes. She found the largest one and brought it down to Ant. He opened it and immediately tried to stuff Moe's body inside. After several attempts, he realized he was just too big to fit inside the suitcase. So, he went with the next best thing and rolled his body inside Aspen's dining room rug.

"You gonna need a new one anyway," he spoke. "I'ma pull my truck up to your garage door, but I'ma need help carrying his body out there," Ant continued.

Ant pulled his Yukon up to Aspen's garage door and opened his trunk. The four of them worked together as they carried Moe's dead weight. Once he was in the trunk, Ant ordered the girls to clean the entire house from top to bottom.

"Be sure to wash all the walls and baseboards. Don't leave no corner untouched," Ant ordered. They nodded their heads and got to work while Ant pulled off down the street.

CHAPTER TEN

Graduation day came and went, and they threw the graduation party of the century for the entire senior class. Several weeks had passed, and although they'd seen Ant on his regular re-up a couple times a week, he hadn't said anything about what he did with Moe's body. They didn't ask any questions either. They hadn't seen any news reports on Moe, and the police hadn't come to their doorstep. They'd gotten away with murder three times over, and the average person wouldn't be able to tell they had anything going on. They went on with their everyday teenage lives as if they were not robbery committing murderers.

"When we gonna hit our next lick, and who y'all think it should be?" Justice asked as the three of them sat in Aspen's living room, eating pizza.

It had been weeks since their last hit, and although they

were nowhere near broke, Justice wanted to hit as many spots as she could before they completely stopped. The money was coming quickly, and Justice was allowing the thrill of robbing to control her. "Bitch, we ain't doing no hits no time soon. We all made the decision to stop until shit cooled off," Aspen replied.

"Shit is cold as a witch's tit in the hood. Ain't nobody looking for us. We good out here."

"Nah, I ain't with it. You ain't the one that got the bodies. Me and Aspen do. That last hit we did went all the way wrong, and you just wanna get back to it like that shit never happened? Fuck wrong with you? That nigga was about to shoot you. You could be dead right now," Brianna exclaimed, not believing she was hearing Justice correctly.

"But he didn't shoot me, and I'm not dead. I'm alive. Here to see another day and get more money. You know why he couldn't shoot me? It's cause he didn't have a chance to. We got each other's backs. Before that nigga could even raise his gun all the way, you had that nigga on the floor, and Aspen took care of the other one."

Brianna couldn't do anything except shake her head. "Well, I'm not with it. If you can't see that we need to cool off then I don't know what to tell you. But what I do know is I won't be robbing nobody for a good minute."

Anger shot through Justice's body as she listened to Brianna speak. Aspen saying no was one thing. However, Brianna was her cousin, her flesh and blood. Justice felt that if anybody should have her back, it should be Brianna. There she was though, standing alone with her girls not with her.

"So, y'all really gonna make me stand alone?"

"You not standing alone. We right here with you. All we sayin' is that we need to wait a while before we do our next hit. Ain't none of us hurtin' for no money, so what's the rush? The spots ain't going nowhere, and we still got bricks to sell from the last hit. We good so let's just be good," Aspen reasoned.

"You know what? Y'all got it. I'm trippin'. We can sit down for however long y'all want," Justice agreed, and they dropped the conversation. She could understand why her girls didn't want to do another mission just yet. So, she decided she would side with the majority vote for now. However, when her money did start getting low, they would have no choice but to complete another mission. There was no way Justice was going back to broke. She would rob them niggas herself before she allowed that to happen. She would give her friends a few more weeks before she would bring the topic up again, hoping that by then, their minds would have changed.

BRIANNA'S BIRTHDAY party was lit. She had a large tent set up on the island by the beach, which she decorated in a Hawaiian theme. There were several other smaller tents around the main tent, all with various things inside from drink and food stations to massage and pedicure bars. There were several hookah stations that Brianna also had incorporated with the Hawaiian theme. She had a DJ bumping all the good shit, keeping the vibes going as the partygoers enjoyed themselves.

Brianna had spared no expense to ensure her eighteenth birthday was everything she wanted and more. They ate good, having their choice of different cuisines from different countries. Brianna had a table full of gifts under one of the tents, and partygoers added to it as they arrived. When Ant pulled up, she knew it wouldn't be any different.

"Happy birthday, Bri." Ant spoke, handing her a gift bag.

"Thank you, Uncle."

Brianna couldn't wait to see what Ant had gotten her. So, instead of putting his gift on the table with all the others, she decided to open it. Reaching into the gift bag, she pulled out a JBW box. When she opened it, she found it was the same Mink PS that she was going to get for herself. She smiled from ear to ear as she wrapped her arms around Ant's neck.

"Thank you so much, Uncle Ant. I love it." Brianna beamed.

"I'm glad you like it," Ant replied, smiling at his niece. He walked up closer to her, lowering his voice so that only she could hear. "I need to talk to you and yo girls. Come roll with me for a minute."

Brianna agreed before gathering Justice and Aspen. The three of them got into Ant's Yukon and drove away. "What's up, Ant? What you need to talk to us about?" Brianna asked.

"I got a business proposition for y'all. I been buying keys

from y'all for a minute, and it's been makin' us all money. But what if I said I could triple that shit?"

"We listenin'," Justice uttered, wanting to know exactly what he meant.

"I got some niggas that want to cop some weight. How much do y'all think y'all can get?" he asked.

"We got five bricks left. We can sell them to you tonight," Aspen informed.

"Yeah, the five bricks is cool. I got somebody that wants five right now. But we gonna need more than just that. I don't know who y'all connect is, and I don't need to know. But do y'all think y'all can get forty keys? If y'all can get that for us to start off with, I can make them forty keys sixty keys. That will put us on real nice."

The girls knew they would stand to make a lot of money if they went into business with Ant. However, neither Brianna nor Aspen were ready to go back to hitting licks. Before they could speak, Justice opened her mouth.

"We can get it. Hell, we can get way more than that."

"Cool. The more y'all can get, the more money we gonna make," Ant stated.

Aspen wanted to slap Justice in those same lips the words had just left. This was supposed to be a group decision, and as a group, they'd decided to lay low. Now here Justice was, making decisions for all of them. She looked over at Brianna, and their unspoken words let each other know they both felt the same way.

"Bitch, why the fuck did you tell him that?" Aspen asked as soon as they exited Ant's truck.

"Bitch, cause it's true. We can get all the weight he needs. We can make way more money than we been making if we go into business with Ant. Didn't you hear him say he can triple our money?"

"And didn't you hear us say we were laying low? Fuck is wrong with you, making decisions for everyone? We make decisions as a team. There is no leader in this group," Aspen informed.

"Oh, you mean the way y'all made decisions for me when y'all decided to stop? I didn't want to do that shit, but y'all decided, so I went along with it. Now, it's y'all turn." Justice walked off, not wanting to take the conversation any further. Her mind was made up, and nothing was going to stop her from getting this money, not even her home girls.

"As much as I don't want to do another mission just yet, and don't like the way Justice is going about things, you have to admit we would make a lot of money with Ant. And we can trust him. I feel much safer having him partner with us," Brianna reasoned.

Aspen knew they were both right about the money. Working with Ant would make them rich quickly. However, that didn't take away from the fact that they had already made a group decision. Now it was Aspen's turn to go with the majority vote.

"What up doe, Ant?" Shanté greeted, walking up to the

car. She'd seen the girls take a ride with him, and her mother's intuition was set off. Shanté wasn't green to the game at all. She'd noticed her daughter spending a lot of money lately, and she knew no fast food job would allow her to have that much money. Shanté knew how Ant made his money, and she'd hoped her daughter wasn't in the game. However, when she saw Brianna get in his car and drive off with Aspen and Justice, she knew what was up. "Where y'all go?" she continued.

"Hey, Shanté. I just wanted to have a talk with my niece. She turned eighteen today, and this world is a crazy place. I wanted her to know that Unc got her back if she ever needed me. I got your back too. Long as my brother behind that wall, I got you for anything," Ant spoke.

Shanté nodded her head and looked over at Brianna. She knew Ant wasn't telling the whole truth, but she wouldn't have that conversation at Brianna's party. "Well, alright then. I hope you're staying. Why don't you grab a plate?"

"You already know a nigga gon' eat," Ant chuckled.

Shanté looked over at Brianna one more time, looking deep into her eyes, trying to read her face. When she didn't see anything out of the ordinary, she walked off and went back to the dance floor.

"Bitch, did you see the way she was looking at you? She knows something," Aspen suggested.

"Knows something like what? You just being paranoid," Justice spoke.

Brianna knew her mother, so she definitely knew Aspen was on to something. She just didn't know how much her mother knew or what she thought she knew. *Ain't no way she know we was hittin' licks. She would have been said somethin'. She wouldn't be able to hold that shit in,* Brianna thought. "She just probably being nosy and wants to know what Ant said to me," Brianna shrugged it off.

THE NEXT MORNING, Brianna woke up early. They'd planned a meeting at Aspen's house to talk about their next mission. She'd just gotten dressed and was downstairs in the kitchen, making herself breakfast, when Shanté joined her.

"Did you enjoy your party yesterday?" Shanté asked, pouring herself a cup of coffee.

"Yes, I did. I had so much fun. Everything was perfect from the decorations to the food."

"Yeah, it was. Yesterday was beautiful and seemed like it cost a lot of money to put together. I know for sure it was way more than the thousand dollars I gave you," Shanté stated, eyeing Brianna, waiting for her response.

"It was more, but I had some money saved. Plus, Justice and Aspen helped out a lot," Brianna lied. The truth was she hadn't even spent the money her mother had given her. She planned to drop it back in her purse at a later time. Her party was well over ten thousand dollars, and Brianna had paid for everything with her own money.

"They don't have jobs either. And even if y'all did have jobs, the amount of money you spendin' ain't coming from no McDonald's," Shanté spoke.

"Mama, what exactly are you saying to me?" Brianna asked, wanting Shanté to cut to the point.

"I'm asking you where you getting all this money from. For the last few months, you been havin' yo pockets full, buyin' all kinds of new shit, expensive shit, and I wanna know where all this money is comin' from," Shanté pressed.

"I just told you where I got it from, Ma."

"And I'm telling you it didn't. You walkin' around here with too much money to be workin' a little afterschool job. You literally just graduated. I'm not stupid, Brianna. Now, I know you just turned eighteen, but you are still in my house. So, you better not be sellin' no damn drugs with Ant."

Brianna looked at Shanté in shock as she tried to come up with her next lie. *Shit, she does know.* "Ma, I'm not sellin' no drugs. I been savin' my money up for senior year and my birthday. We all have. It only looks like we spent more than we did because we know how to make it look that way. A lot of that stuff was DIY. We spent hours at Aspen's house putting together most of those decorations by hand," Brianna lied.

Shanté looked into her daughter's eyes, trying to detect a lie. She sighed and gave a half smile. "I just don't want you to get caught up in that life. Nothing good comes out of it. The money comes fast, and it might seem like you livin' yo best life, but when that downfall comes, that shit hits hard. Look at yo daddy. He in jail and ain't never getting out. Or what about Aspen's parents? They got it even worse. Her daddy used to run these streets. Now both him and her mama are in the ground."

"I know all that, Ma, and I'm tellin' you I'm not sellin' no drugs. Calm down, Ma. You worryin' too much for nothin'," Brianna spoke, walking over to her mother and kissing her on the cheek. Brianna felt horrible for lying to her mother. They were extremely close seeing how it was just the two of them. However, Brianna knew there was no way she could tell her mother anything about her secret life.

Shanté nodded her head, believing her daughter. Brianna set two plates of eggs and bacon down at the kitchen island, and they both ate breakfast together. Brianna made a mental note to begin looking for her own place. If they were going to be pushing major weight, she was going to have to move out of her mother's house, especially now that she seemed to question what she was doing.

CHAPTER ELEVEN

A year had passed since the girls had gone into business with Ant, and things couldn't have been better. At only nineteen years old, all three of them were multi-millionaires. They had expanded their business and started hitting fentanyl and meth spots as well. No matter what they came back with, Ant could always find a way to sell it, making them all more money than they had ever seen in their lives.

Justice lived in a four-bedroom home in Farmington Hills. She'd met her boyfriend, Cream, eight months ago, and they'd been inseparable ever since. Cream stood six foot two inches tall with dark chocolate skin and a muscular build. He stayed in the gym to keep his chiseled frame, and it was something he took pride in. His locs were always neatly twisted, and tonight, they were pulled back into a low ponytail. Cream was a hustler, but he didn't sell drugs. Cream was a stone-cold scammer, and numbers were his game. He's made millions of dollars with both wire and tax fraud, and that didn't even include his legit businesses. At just twenty-two years old, he was already the first millionaire in his family.

They both stood in their all-white bathroom, at their his and hers sinks, as they got dressed. Justice stood there in her black lace bra and pantie set as she applied her makeup. Cream's dick stiffened as he eyed her small waist that led to her wide hips and plump ass. Justice had opted out of having a party for her eighteenth birthday and instead took a trip to Dr. Miami and got her body done. She looked like an Instagram model by the way she was caked up, and she was far from that little broke girl that lived in the projects. She'd done a 180 in life and was proud of her come up. Justice had made a name for herself in the streets of Detroit. Not only was she still hitting licks with her girls, but she'd also used some of that money to open her own hair salon and clothing boutique, quickly making herself a hood celebrity.

Cream admired Justice's hustle. It was sexy to him and part of the reason he knew he had to make her his. He walked up to Justice from behind, grabbing her breasts in his hands and placing gentle kisses on her neck. She moaned slightly, throwing her head back onto Cream's shoulder as she enjoyed the feeling.

"Baby, we gotta go. Bri wants to introduce me to her new

man, and she gonna kill me if we late to this dinner," Justice moaned as she closed her eyes.

"We got time," Cream whispered as he trailed kisses down her spine. He got down on his knees, bending Justice over, before sliding her panties to one side. He swirled his wet tongue around Justice's clitoris, and she moaned out loud. His manhood hardened with each lick. "Damn, you taste so good," Cream moaned, licking her as if she was a popsicle on a hundred degree day.

Justice's legs began to tremble as her orgasm neared. She grabbed Cream's head, pushing him deeper into her love box, as she reached her peak, quenching Cream's thirst as she rained her sweet juices into his mouth. He stood to his feet, sliding his manhood inside of her tight wetness.

"Shit, baby," Justice uttered as Cream filled her.

Cream pumped harder and faster, grabbing Justice's face, pulling her into a sloppy kiss. They both moaned as they released at the same time, now feeling spent. "Now, come on. We gotta hurry up and take another shower, so we can get dressed for real this time," Justice ordered.

Justice and Creamed pulled up to Brianna's house with five minutes to spare. "I told you we had time," Cream joked as he got out the car.

They walked up to Brianna's door, and Justice rang the doorbell. Aspen opened the door, already knowing it was Justice. "Hey, girl," she greeted. "Brianna's back there in the kitchen, putting the finishing touches on dinner."

Justice and Cream walked into Brianna's luxurious three-bedroom home. Brianna had hired a decorator to come in and decorate her home from top to bottom with the most high-end pieces she could find. She had tens of thousands of dollars' worth of African art on her wall, and huge plants that hung from the ceiling, and white furniture throughout.

"Hey, bitch, you got it smellin' good as hell up in here," Justice greeted, walking into the kitchen.

"Hey, y'all, dinner will be ready in a few," Brianna informed, taking a pan of crab stuffed shrimp from the oven.

"Do you need help with anything?" Justice asked.

"Nope, everything is done. I just got to plate it. Y'all can have a seat at the dining room table," Brianna replied. "Thank y'all for coming," Brianna continued.

"Of course we was gon' be here. You said you wanted us to meet your new boo. Now where is this mystery man?" Aspen asked.

"He went to the liquor store to get us a couple bottles of wine. He'll be back in a few."

"I'm back now." A deep baritone spoke before a tall, light-skinned man with a full beard entered the room. He stood about six foot four and was about three hundred pounds of solid muscle. His low cut waves were deep, and he had on so much gold jewelry that he resembled Pac on the *I Get Around* music video.

"Loke, this is my cousin, Justice, and my home girl,

Aspen. And that's Brianna's man, Cream. Y'all, this is Loke," Brianna introduced.

Loke said hi and shook everyone's hands as they took a seat at the dining room table. Brianna had outdone herself with the cooking, making steak, lobster, and crab stuffed shrimp with garlic mashed potatoes and asparagus on the side. She even made strawberry lemon tarts for dessert.

"So, how did the two of y'all meet? You must be something really special because Bri kept you from us for a minute now, and we tell each other everything," Aspen spoke.

"We met at the grocery store. I went to go grab some watermelon, and there, standing in the produce section, was the most beautiful woman I'd ever seen in my life. I knew I had to introduce myself when I saw her, and I'm glad I did because here we are now," Loke spoke.

"Aww, so it was like love at first sight?" Justice asked.

"That's exactly what it was," Loke replied, taking Brianna's hand into his and smiling at her.

"Y'all so cute." Aspen smiled.

They all sat around the table after dinner, getting to know one another over glasses of wine. Brianna told the ladies to join her in her bedroom. "Loke, this will give you and Cream a chance to get to know each other man to man. Y'all gonna be around each other a lot more now," Brianna informed.

"Come on, bro. We can go in the basement. We don't wanna hear they girl talk anyway," Loke joked, leading Cream downstairs.

"So, Ant came over today and said he needs forty more keys. I'm thinking we can hit Reese's spot and get double that easy," Brianna informed.

"He got two spots, one on the west and one on the east. I say we hit the one on the west side. That one seems to make way more money," Aspen spoke.

"Yeah, you right about that," Justice agreed.

They agreed to meet at Aspen's house at nine that next morning. Justice had a standing Saturday night date with Cream, so she needed to hit the lick early, so she could make it to her one o'clock nail appointment that she knew would take three hours. After about thirty more minutes of standard girl talk, it was time to go home.

"What you think about Loke?" Justice asked Cream on the ride home.

"I just met him. I don't have no opinion on the nigga either way," Cream spoke.

"Yeah, but y'all had a one on one. Do you think y'all will be cool?" Justice pressed.

"Baby, I don't know. We had a cool conversation over a glass of Hennessey, but it was one conversation. I ain't best friends with the nigga," Cream joked.

"I know," Justice laughed. "I just got this vision of us all on baecation together on some tropical island."

"We don't need them for us to go on a tropical island. We can do that whenever you want to."

"I know, baby. I just have a vision of going on vacation

with my girls and our men. That's why we need to find Aspen a boo. She the only one of us that don't have one. I know you got some home boys that you can introduce her to," Justice suggested.

"Nah, baby, I'm a real nigga. I ain't 'bout to be playing Cupid. That's lame," Cream spoke.

"Fine then, Cream. Just crush all my dreams just like that," she joked. They made their way back home, finishing what they started before they left.

"WHERE YOU GOING, BABY?" Cream asked, watching Justice dress in a two-piece, baby blue, cropped sweatsuit.

"I'm going shopping with my girls to find something to wear for our date tonight. Then, I got a nail appointment after that," she halfway lied.

"Oh, you getting sexy for Daddy, huh?" Cream got out of bed and wrapped his arms around Justice, kissing her passionately.

"You know I'ma stay sexy for you, Daddy."

With that, Justice left her house, heading to Aspen's. When she arrived, she saw that Brianna was already there. She rang the doorbell and walked inside when the door was opened.

"Good morning. It's a great day to make this money," Aspen greeted.

"Yes, it is, and I'm ready to get to it," Justice replied.

"I got us some new outfits. Justice, yo ass is getting thicker by the day, so she gonna need something to hide all that shit," Aspen joked as she pulled the new larger sized clothing out of the Macy's bag and handed them to Justice.

"Girl, my man loves this phat ass. Dr. Miami did his thang!" Justice spoke, slapping herself on the ass.

Aspen laughed, walking away to change into her disguise. They made their way to Reese's spot, parking right in front of the house. "Y'all ready?" Justice asked.

"We stay ready," Aspen and Brianna spoke in unison. The three ladies got out the car and walked up to the front door. Justice knocked on the door, and when it opened, they all burst inside.

"Run dat shit, nigga," Brianna spoke, placing her gun up to the man's head.

Just like that, they were in and out the spot with three duffle bags full of money and weight. They drove back to Aspen's house, only to change clothes and cars, then were right back out again. They took the fifty keys they'd just stole right to Ant's house for their profit.

"Alright, y'all. I gotta go. I gotta get to my nail appointment," Justice stated before taking her cut of the profits and walking out the door.

OVER THE NEXT SEVERAL MONTHS, the girls had been putting in major work and pulling in major money. They had hit a lick a week for the past four months and had been working harder than ever. It was Super Bowl Sunday, and Brianna and Loke were hosting a Super Bowl party. Loke had invited several of his friends to come, including Cream. They'd became friends, often getting together on Sundays to watch the football game together. Brianna had, of course, invited Aspen and Justice because she refused to be the only woman at the party.

They were all sitting around Brianna's huge living room, watching the game, when the doorbell rang. Loke got up to answer it then walked back inside the living room with a tall, brown-skinned, skinny man. He introduced him to Brianna as his cousin, Quan.

"Hey, Quan, it's nice to finally meet you. I've heard a lot about you. These is my cousin, Justice, and our home girl, Aspen," Brianna introduced.

Aspen smiled and extended her hand. He smiled back at her when they locked eyes, and Aspen felt her heart skip a beat. "It's nice to meet you, Aspen," Quan spoke, shaking Aspen's hand gently.

"Same here," Aspen cooed.

"We bout to get back to this game," Loke said, motioning Quan to join him on the sectional with the rest of the guys.

"Bitch, that nigga is fine as hell. That's his cousin? Why I ain't never seen him around before?" Aspen asked.

"He just moved back here from Baltimore a few weeks ago," Brianna informed.

"Do he got a girl?" Aspen inquired.

"I'm not sure, but if you get to know him, you might find out."

Aspen chuckled because she knew Brianna was right. She walked over to the microwave and pulled out one of the Wingstop containers and filled a plate with wings before walking over to the sectional where the men sat.

"Here you go, fellas. I thought y'all might need a refill on those wings," Aspen stated, winking her eye at Quan as she sat the plate on the table. Quan smiled at her before she turned around and walked away.

"Girl, what the fuck was that?" Brianna laughed.

"Bitch, you know the quickest way to a man's heart is through his stomach."

Several moments later, Aspen and Quan were inside Brianna's dining room, having a conversation. She found out that Quan was indeed single with no attachments. Aspen found Quan to be very interesting. He explained to her that he was in real estate and owned several properties in both Michigan and Baltimore. By the end of the night, they had exchanged numbers and made plans to go out to dinner with each other the following night.

Aspen made her way back home, smiling from ear to ear. There was something special about Quan. She just couldn't put her finger on it. She hadn't even talked to another man since Moe, and the fact that she wanted to give Quan her time said a lot about him. She wanted to get to know him better and see what could happen between them.

. . .

THE NEXT DAY, Aspen spent hours, trying on outfits. She wanted to find the perfect one for her date with Quan. After several attempts, she finally settled on a black, one piece, spaghetti strapped jumpsuit. The top was lace and see-through, so she wore a black, strapless bra underneath, not wanting to reveal too much on the first date. She kept her makeup look simple with soft natural glam and a red lip for a pop of color. She washed and flat ironed her customized 613 lace-front bob with dark brown roots and installed it. Aspen wore her three-piece, gold Fendi set as her jewelry of choice. While both her shoes and bag were Chanel, her fragrance of choice was Baccarat Rouge 540. She finished her look with a black fur jacket, and she knew she looked good. She looked and smelled like money and was eager to see Quan.

Her doorbell rang exactly at eight o'clock, and Aspen was impressed by his promptness. She sprayed herself once more with her perfume before she made her way to the door.

"Wow, you look beautiful," Quan complimented, smiling at Aspen. He handed her a dozen red roses, and Aspen's heart melted.

"Thank you," she replied, allowing Quan entry to her home. She smelled his Oud For Greatness cologne as he passed by her, and she smiled. She loved when a man smelled good. His black Balmain jeans and sweater fit his body like they were tailor made for him. The Gucci link chain and two carat diamond earring he wore stood out to Aspen. She knew he had to be getting money on her level because the Gucci link chain was more expensive than a regular Cuban link that everyone had.

Quan had made reservations for them at Joe Muer Seafood, and neither of them wanted to be late. Aspen hadn't eaten all day, being too busy trying to find the perfect outfit to wear. She was starving and loved seafood, so she was more than ready to eat. She grabbed her purse, and they walked out the door.

CHAPTER TWELVE

Over the next few months, Aspen and Quan had grown extremely close, seeing each other almost every day. They'd made their relationship official, going from just casual dating to giving each other the title of boyfriend and girlfriend, and they were both happy. They had even moved in together, both living in Aspen's home. They were cuddled up in Aspen's bed one Saturday afternoon when Aspen's phone rang.

"Hello?" she answered.

"Bitch, what you doing?" Justice screamed into the phone.

"Nothing, watching a movie with Quan. What up doe?"

"Bitch, you and Quan get packed. We all going to Punta Cana. We leave Friday morning," Justice informed.

"Bitch, what the hell are you talkin' 'bout?

"Girl, my man, my man, my man… He got us all first class

tickets to Punta Cana. And bitch, it's all inclusive. We got private villas and everything. This shit gon' be lit!"

"I know you fuckin' lyin'? And we leave this Friday? Oh, I gotta go shopping," Aspen stated, jumping up out of bed.

"Let me know when you ready and we can go together."

Aspen ended the call and got back in the bed with Quan, telling him the good news. "Cream tryna show out, takin' us all to Punta Cana and shit. We gon' go though," Quan joked.

"I gotta get some new clothes and wigs for this trip. This bout to be fun as hell. I've never been out of the country before," Aspen stated.

FRIDAY CAME QUICKLY, and the three couples all met at DTW to board their flight. This was Aspen's first time on a plane, and she had to admit she was a bit nervous. She'd heard about plane crashes and planes disappearing out of the sky, never to be seen again. Quan, being over twenty-one, got a glass of champagne, which he gave to Aspen, hoping it would calm her down.

"Everything is gon' be fine, babe. Just relax and take a nap. By the time you wake up, we will be there," Quan suggested.

"I'm trying to relax, but it's not working. Can you get me another glass of champagne?"

Quan nodded and motioned the flight attendant over to him. Once he got his glass, he handed it to Aspen when nobody was looking. She drank it down before laying her head down on Quan's shoulder. She closed her eyes and tried to relax, thinking about the beautiful water she was about to swim in.

When they landed, Cream had a Sprinter pick them up from the airport and take them to their villas. Each couple had their own villa, and they were all side by side and overlooked the water. They were in pure paradise for the next week, and they couldn't wait to enjoy themselves.

"Here's everyone's room keys. Today is a chill day, nothing much planned other than dinner tonight. Tomorrow is when the vacation really begins, so make sure y'all rest up." Cream spoke.

They all agreed and went into their villas. Aspen immediately went to the bathroom to take a shower. She wanted to wash the flight off and go lay on the beach to catch some much-needed sunlight. The water was the bluest she'd ever seen before in her life, and she was eager to feel it on her body.

"Is it room for me in there with you?" Quan asked, stepping into the shower with Aspen.

Aspen smiled, wrapping her arms around his neck, and kissing him passionately. "We bout to have the best week of our lives," she whispered.

"One of the best weeks. It's nothing but greatness for us from here on out."

Aspen smiled, knowing he was telling the truth. She

planned to travel a lot with Quan. She was in love again, and this time, she knew it was real. Quan had come in and added to her life, and she was grateful that he was hers.

Quan cuffed Aspen's ass as he kissed her back, tongues dancing as both their hearts raced. It didn't matter how many times they'd done that same act. Each time felt like the first. Quan was Aspen's person, and she was glad he'd finally found her.

They made love right there under the rain shower, giving each other exactly what they needed. After making their way into the bedroom area, Aspen changed into her new Gucci bikini that she'd gotten for the trip.

"You coming to the beach with me?" Aspen asked, placing a large straw hat on her head to shield her face from the sun.

"Well, I damn sure ain't gon' stay in here and let you go down there lookin' like you lookin' alone. Damn, Aspen, you gon' have me killin' niggas out here in Punta Cana," Quan spoke.

"Boy, you crazy," Aspen laughed.

Quan changed into a pair of Gucci shorts and a beater before they left the villa, heading down to the beach. They found two empty beach chairs and took a seat.

"Hello, can I offer you anything to drink?" the waiter asked, walking over to Quan and Aspen.

"Yes, I'll take a Corona with lime," Quan ordered.

"And I'll have a Mango margarita," Aspen said.

The waiter walked off and went to place their drink orders.

"I think I like Punta Cana already. He didn't even check my ID," Aspen said.

"It wouldn't matter if he did. You are legal to drink here at nineteen," Quan informed.

The waiter was back just a few short moments later with their drinks. They sipped while they relaxed and enjoyed the view.

CREAM HAD a tent set up for them on the beach. The candlelit dinner table was decorated beautifully with several bouquets of tropical flowers. The centerpieces were made of huge seashell covered vases that housed more flowers and candles. There were torches lit all around to light their way on the dark beach. The entire scene was romantic, and the ladies were impressed that Cream had put it all together. The three couples sat around the table and were served by men and women dressed in all-white. The entire scene was a vibe, and everyone felt it.

"I'd like to thank everyone for coming on our first annual couples' trip… or what my baby would call it, our baecation. I hope everyone's villa are up to their standards. And if it's not, please let me know," Cream announced.

"Everything is good. I've never even been out the country, so all this shit all new to a nigga," Loke replied while everyone else agreed.

"Good. Tomorrow, we have a beach day planned. I rented

us a few jet skis and a yacht. I also set up a time for us to swim with the dolphins."

"Nigga, what? What hood you from? Now the jet skis are cool, but I ain't swimming with no damn dolphins," Quan responded. "Hood niggas don't do that type of shit. Hell, Black people period don't do that shit. You ain't bout to kill me," he continued.

Cream chuckled and nodded his head. "I get it, my guy. But Justice picked that out, so we all going. Anyone that does not wanna swim with the dolphins can just stay on the boat or just ride the jet skis, no big deal."

"Come on, baby. Swimming with dolphins sounds fun. Just try it with me," Aspen urged.

"I'ma go on the boat with y'all, and I'ma ride the jet skis. But I'm not gon' promise that I'ma swim with no damn sea animals. That ain't my thing."

The entire table laughed with all the men feeling the same way Quan did. None of them wanted to swim with the dolphins but would all go because their women wanted to.

"The night is still young, so after dinner, we can go out to one of the clubs on the resort. Let's all raise our glasses and toast to a wonderful trip and all the memories that we gon' make," Cream spoke.

They all raised their glasses, clinking them together as they toasted. They enjoyed their dinner and went to the club after. They had a blast, and it was only the first night there.

The next day, they all went to swim with the dolphins as

planned. It was so beautiful and peaceful on the water that everyone, including Quan, got into the water. They drank champagne and ate lobster as they all enjoyed the fruits of their labor.

THE WEEK WENT BY FAST, and the vacation was now over. It was now back to business as usual. The girls were gone for a week, so they hadn't hit any licks. Ant was almost out of product and needed to re-up fast. The three of them sat around Aspen's dining room table, setting up the three licks they planned to hit that week.

Each one of the hustlers' spots would bring them major weight. Ant was selling keys faster than they could get them. So, they thought if they hit multiple licks in a week, it would give them a head start advantage. The first lick was going to be that next day. Mook was a well-known hustler in the city, and they knew he would bring them major weight.

That next day, they hit Mook as planned. Everything went smoothly as they were in and out the house within five minutes with all the money and weight they had. They took the keys to Ant as usual. Aspen's phone rang as soon as they pulled out of Ant's driveway. She looked down and saw it was Quan, and she swiped the talk button.

"Where you at?" Quan asked.

"Out with Justice and Brianna. What's up?"

"I just wanted you to know you got some mail at the

house. I left it on the kitchen counter for you. I'm gon' be gone for a few hours, so I might not be here when you get home. Do you wanna go out to dinner tonight, or do you wanna order in?"

"We can stay in tonight if you don't mind. Order food and watch a movie or something. I just wanna chill," Aspen replied.

"Cool, sounds good to me. I'll see you when I get home," Quan spoke before ending the call.

When Aspen walked inside her house, she went straight to the kitchen to retrieve her mail. Aspen was surprised to find that it was a letter from her sister, Cove. She hadn't written Aspen in months, so she was happy to finally hear from her. The letter stated that Cove wanted Aspen to come and visit her that following week. Aspen couldn't have been happier. She hadn't seen her sister in years and couldn't wait for the visit.

CHAPTER THIRTEEN

spen sat in the visitation room of the prison as she waited for Cove to walk in. Her heart beat fast as she became nervous to see her sister. When she finally walked inside, Aspen smiled as soon as she laid eyes on her. Even though Cove was in her orange prison issued jumpsuit with corn rolls in her hair, her beauty was still breathtaking. Aspen stood to her feet, running over to Cove, and hugging her tightly.

"No touching, inmate," one of the COs yelled. Cove let Aspen go and took her seat at the table.

"Cove, I'm so happy that you finally let me come see you. I've missed you so much. It's been crazy out here without you."

"You look so beautiful; my baby sister is all grown up for real. I miss you too, Aspen, and I hope you understand why I did what I did. I couldn't let you be the one in here. This shit is rough, and I would have much rather it be me behind the wall than you. I wouldn't know what I would do if I had to worry about you being in here." Cove dropped her head in shame. "I should have protected you. I knew what Red was capable of, and no matter what they said or did, I should have never left you there with them. This shit is on me. That's why I took it," Cove continued.

"Cove, none of this is your fault, so don't blame yourself. We don't get to pick our lives, sis. We just gotta live them the best way we can. Shit not all bad for me anymore. Life is actually good, real good. And when you get outta here, it's gonna get better for us both."

Cove smiled, happy to hear her sister say she was doing good. Although this was the first time she'd seen Aspen since she'd went to prison, Shanté had kept her up to date with the goings-on of Aspen's life. She knew everything about her sister, but she wanted to hear it all from her firsthand.

"So, tell me what's new in your life. Do you still have any of the money that I left you?" Cove asked.

"I'm good on money, sis. I even got you some put up for you for when you get out. I'ma set you up real nice, and you ain't gon' have to worry 'bout shit."

"You working?" Cove asked.

"Not for nobody else. I started my own lip gloss line with some of the money you left me, and it turned into a six figure business," Aspen lied.

She didn't want to lie to her sister, but there was no way she was going to tell Cove what she really did to get her money. Cove had her own shit to worry about, and Aspen knew that if she told her, that would only add to it.

"So, who's this new nigga that you been seeing lately? Shanté told me that all y'all got boyfriends."

"His name is Quan, and he's so good to me. He treats me like a queen. I really couldn't ask for a better man by my side."

"Aww, that's sweet. I love that for you, sis. How did y'all meet?" Cove asked.

"He's Brianna's boyfriend's cousin. We met at a Super Bowl party they had and been together ever since."

"That's good, long as he treating you right then that's all that matters to me. I'm glad you happy, sis. I can tell that you truly are. I can see it all in your face," Cove responded.

The sisters sat there for the next thirty minutes, catching up on everything that Cove missed out on being in prison. Hearing that Aspen had changed her life around for the good gave Cove hope of a better life after prison.

"Can I come back next week and see you?" Aspen asked once the CO instructed them the visit was over.

"Yeah, I'd like that."

Aspen watched as Cove walked in chains out of the visitation room. She hated the way the system failed them, the same way they always failed the Black community. *The state placed us in the home with a raping ass pedophile, the same pedophile that killed our parents. Then, when we retaliate, the state placed Cove in prison. They the real problem if you ask me.*

Aspen walked out the prison and back to her car. She had two missed calls, one from Quan and the other from Justice. She called Quan back first, and when he didn't answer, she called Justice.

"Hey, girl, did you go see Cove yet?" Justice asked as soon as she pressed the talk button.

"Yeah, I'm on my way home. The visit went good. She wants me to come back and see her next week."

"Good, I'm happy to hear that... On another note, Cream's birthday is next weekend, and I wanna throw him a dawg ass party," Justice informed.

"Oh, that sounds dope. If you need help planning, let me know."

"Girl, I'ma hire somebody to do all that shit. All I'm doing is paying and showing up," Justice laughed.

"I should have known," Aspen chuckled. "Well, you know me and Quan gonna be there."

"Oh, I know. And I know this party gon' be some racks. So, you already know what we gon' have to do," Justice stated.

Aspen already knew that meant they needed to hit a few licks, and she was down for it. Seeing Cove in that prison suit for something she'd done put a fire under her. She had to make sure Cove was up and stayed there. There was nothing she wouldn't do to assure that happened, including robbing every fucking drug dealer in the state of Michigan.

"Call Bri and let's meet at my house to plan something," Aspen suggested.

"Cool, I'll text her now."

They met at Aspen's house and planned on hitting three more licks before Cream's party that following Saturday with the first hit being the very next day.

CHAPTER FOURTEEN

They were two licks in for the week with their last hit being in Kalamazoo that next day. Aspen drove down the freeway with her radio on blast on her way to visit Cove. It was a hot summer's day in the city, and the sun was shining. It was a good day, and Aspen was happy to go see her sister. When she arrived at the prison, she parked and left everything but her driver's license inside the car.

Once she was inside the visitation room, she sat at a table and waited on Cove to arrive. When she walked in, Aspen immediately saw the look of anger on her face. Cove sat in her seat and waited for the CO to walk away before speaking in a low whisper.

"Aspen, what the fuck you out here doing in these streets?"

"What you talkin' bout?" Aspen asked, confused.

"Aspen, please tell me you not out here hittin' licks on trap houses?"

Aspen was flabbergasted. She had no idea her sister knew anything about what she was doing. Hell, nobody knew about the hits but herself, Justice, and Brianna. *How the fuck does she know this?* Aspen asked herself.

"What? I ain't hittin' licks on nobody. Who the hell told you that?"

"It don't matter who told me. I'm telling you that if I know, then someone else knows. You need to be careful. These niggas out here ain't to be played with. You hit the wrong one, and it could fuck you up," Cove warned.

Aspen's eyes widened at the realization. She thought their disguises had done the job. Now that she was in a prison speaking with her sister, she realized she'd been wrong. She tried to hide her surprise from her sister, but Cove was far from dumb. So, she knew once she saw the look on Aspen face that it was true.

"Look, baby sis, I know you got the hustle in yo heart. You got that shit from Daddy. It's in me too. But Daddy was smart. You can't be sloppy with that shit. For me to even know this shit means you was sloppy somewhere."

"I thought I was being smart," Aspen whispered.

She thought they'd done everything right. They'd put on disguises, and they'd went in early in the morning when not many people were at the spot. They'd even got a car designated for hits only. Yet and still, someone had found out about them.

"You gotta be careful, sis. I'm not gonna tell you not to do it cause I know you gotta get yo money. But be smart about the shit. Whatever way you was doing it, switch that shit up. This a dangerous game you playing, so keep yo circle small."

Cove wished she could rewind time, and go back to the day her parents were murdered, so she could have kept them alive. If she could, none of this would even be happening. She hated that her sister had to hit licks just to get a bag.

When Aspen left the prison, she immediately called Justice and Brianna and asked them to meet her at her house. She needed to let them know they'd been found out. They needed to come up with a different plan by tomorrow if they were still going to hit the lick in Kalamazoo.

When she arrived home, she saw that Quan's car was parked in the driveway. She knew she couldn't have the conversation she needed to have with her girls while he was there. So, she called them and told them to meet her at the park around the corner from her house.

When she got there, she parked next to Brianna's Honda Civic and got out her truck. She got into the backseat and immediately began telling them about her visit with Cove.

"What the fuck you mean she knows? Who the fuck told her, and how do they know it's us?" Brianna asked.

"I don't know who told her, but what I do know is that our cover's been blown."

"We gotta move different, switch some shit up for the Kalamazoo hit, then slow down for a minute after that," Justice suggested. "Let's do the Kalamazoo hit late tomorrow night instead of in the morning. If anybody expecting us, they expect us to come in the morning. Let's get another car too. That car probably been spotted," she continued.

"Yeah, we can do that. But after this hit, we gotta stop for a minute. We just gon' have to tell Ant this gon' be his last shipment for a while," Aspen spoke.

"Damn, I wonder who knows it was us. It was probably that nigga, Moe. He probably told one of his home boys or something," Brianna advised.

"I bet it was him too," Justice agreed.

They all agreed to take a break after their next hit. They all had money and could invest what they had into making even more money without hitting licks. When Aspen got back home, she went and took a shower, spending the rest of the night watching movies with Quan.

Aspen, Justice, and Brianna took the forty-five-minute drive to Kalamazoo. They arrived at the spot and parked a couple houses down, turning their headlights off, so they wouldn't be seen. They were dressed in the same disguises they'd always worn. However, they'd gotten another car for this particular hit. Everything was all set, and they were all ready to get it done.

"Y'all ready?" Brianna asked.

"We stay ready," Justice and Aspen replied in unison.

The three of them got out the car, duffle bags in hand. They walked up to the door, and Justice knocked on it. When it opened, the three of them burst inside.

"Run that shit, nigga." Aspen spoke, holding the gun to the goon's head.

He told them exactly where the stash was with no hesitation, and Justice and Brianna went to fill their bags. When they were done and had everything in their duffle bags, they walked out the door. They quickly got inside the car and pulled off down the street, not paying any attention to the car that was following them.

They pulled up to Ant's house and got out the car with the duffle bag that was filled with weight.

"My three favorite ladies. Man, am I happy to see y'all. Any time I see y'all faces, I know we 'bout to make some money," Ant greeted, as they walked inside his home.

"Hey, Ant," all the ladies greeted.

Brianna placed the duffle bag on his table, and Ant opened it, taking out all the bricks one by one. There were thirty in total, and Ant walked into his bedroom to retrieve their money out of his safe. When he returned, he handed the stacks of cash to Brianna, paying for the kilos of cocaine.

"Ant, we got some bad news. This gon' be our last shipment for a while," Aspen informed.

"Fuck you mean? Is something wrong? Why y'all wanna cut off the business? I thought shit was good," he asked, confused about why they wanted to stop making money.

"We ran into a few problems, but it's nothing for you to worry about. You just gon' have to cut the keys you got a few more times than usual. Once we get back on, you will be the first to know," Justice advised.

Ant reluctantly shook his head okay, and the three ladies walked out of his home. When they made their way back to their cars, they parked the car on the side of the road and went their separate ways.

Aspen and Quan walked into the hall where Cream's party was being held. They had on matching white and gold outfits and looked so cute together. It seemed like all of Detroit had come out to help Cream celebrate his birthday. The hall was packed from wall to wall. There were half naked women in gold cages swinging from the ceiling. There were several bars serving free top shelf drinks and several food stations. The casino themed party had several blackjack and poker tables along with a few slot machines. Aspen could tell Justice had spent a pretty penny on this party, and everything had come out nicely.

She scanned the hall, looking for both Justice and Brianna

for several minutes before she found them. They were both standing at one of the bars with Cream and Loke.

"Come on. I see them over there." Aspen pointed, grabbing Quan's hand. They walked over, and Aspen greeted them with a hug.

"Happy birthday, Cream," Aspen said, handing him an envelope. He opened it to find several one hundred dollar bills inside.

"Thanks, y'all. I can definitely do some shit with this," Cream spoke.

"Bro, this shit nice as hell. Y'all got bitches dancing in cages and everything," Quan complimented.

"Yeah, my baby did her thing with this shit," Cream wrapped his arm around Justice's shoulders and kissed her on the forehead.

"Come on, Cream, come smoke this birthday blunt with me," Quan suggested, holding up an already rolled backwood. "Loke, you coming too?" Quan asked.

The guys walked off, heading to a room in the back of the hall. Justice ordered drinks for her and her girls, and they went and sat in the VIP area she'd designated for them.

"Bitch, this party is lit. This better than my eighteenth birthday, and I thought that was the party of the century," Brianna complimented.

"Thanks, I wanted to put something together real nice for Cream. He deserves that shit. That man would give me the world if I asked him to," Justice spoke.

"We all know Cream loves him some Justice. Y'all like couples' goals around the hood," Aspen spoke.

A few moments later, the guys came and joined them in the VIP area. They were bottle girls and servers supplying every food and beverage request they had. They were having a great time and looked like hood royalty.

"I'm bout to go to the bathroom." Brianna leaned over and spoke in Justice's ear.

"I'ma go with you. Aspen, you gotta go to the bathroom?"

Aspen nodded her head, and the three of them got up and walked away. When they got into the bathroom, Brianna reached into her purse and checked her phone. She saw she had several missed calls from her mother. Pressing the call button, she returned her call.

"Briiiiii…" Shanté cried into the phone.

"Ma? What's wrong? Why you crying?" Brianna frantically yelled loudly, catching both Aspen and Justice's attention.

"Ant is dead! He was found shot in his house this afternoon." Shanté was crying so hard she could barely get the words out. Saying Ant was dead out loud was too much for her to bear.

Brianna felt like she was about to pass out as she became lightheaded. She'd just seen Ant yesterday. There was no way he could be dead, not her uncle. A million different scenarios played in her mind of what happened. However, she didn't know anything for certain. All she knew was that her uncle was gone. Tears streamed down her face as she listened to her mother's words.

"What's wrong, Bri?" Aspen mouthed.

Brianna ended the call, telling her mother that she was on her way to her. "Brianna, tell us what happened," Aspen urged.

"Ant is dead. My mama said he was found shot in his house this afternoon."

None of them could believe what was being told to them. Ant might have been Brianna's uncle, but he was cool with all of them. Both Justice and Aspen had genuine love for him. So, the loss of him pained them as well. "I gotta get to my mama's house," Brianna continued.

"We going with you," Justice confirmed.

The three of them walked out the bathroom. Aspen went and told the guys what was going on. Loke immediately jumped up and rushed to Brianna, knowing how close she was to her uncle.

"You want me to go with you?" Quan asked Aspen.

"Nah, you stay here, have a good time. I'll see you when I get home." Aspen kissed Quan on the lips and walked out the door.

When they arrived at Shanté's house, Aspen couldn't believe how sad the scene was. Ant's two sisters were sitting in Shanté's living room, crying hysterically. Shanté was in the kitchen with Brianna's crying grandmother. Aspen wanted to break down at the sight. All this reminded her of the night her parents were killed. She knew the pain of losing a family member all too well, and her heart broke for them.

"I just don't understand why this happened. My son was a good man, would give you the clothes off his back if you needed them. Why would someone just come in his house and shoot him?" Brianna's grandmother cried.

"I'm so sorry, Mama June. I hope the police gets the bastards that did this to him," Shanté spoke.

"Them police officers don't give a damn about what happened to my son. They gon' say it was drug related and leave it at that."

"Drug related? Is that what they told you?" Brianna questioned.

"Yeah, when they called me, I went to his house. I over-heard the officers saying that shit. They not gonna do nothing but let his file collect dust."

Aspen looked over at Justice and motioned for her to follow her. They walked outside, closing the door behind them. "Bitch, do you think he got robbed for the keys we took over there last night?" Aspen asked.

"I was thinking that same thing, but who would do that? Nobody even knew we was working with him. How would anybody know we brought keys over there last night?"

"We don't know what nobody knew. Cove told me someone was on to us. So, what if they knew we was workin' with Ant?" Aspen suggested.

Justice couldn't do anything but shake her head, knowing

that what Aspen was saying was probably true. If, in fact, it was, Justice felt responsible for Ant's death. "I shouldn't have suggested that last hit. When you went and saw Cove and she told you that shit, we should have stopped then," Justice cried. "What if they come back for us? We can't just be sitting ducks," she continued.

"Calm down, Jay. We don't know if it was the Kalamazoo hit or any other lick we've hit. But we gon' have to put our ears to the streets, so we can find out what they saying," Aspen enlightened.

Justice agreed, and they walked back into the home. They all stayed there with the family until the sun came up. By the time Aspen walked inside her home, it was 8:30 in the morning, and she was more than tired. She showered and got in the bed, snuggling up next to Quan.

ANT'S FAMILY sent him off in style, sparing no expense for his funeral services. Greater Grace Temple was filled with people there to pay their respects to Ant. The funeral had to be a closed casket because he was shot in the head, and half of his face was blown off in the process. However, there was dozens of pictures of his smiling face hanging on every wall and beside his casket. There were thousands of white roses in gold vases all around the church, and everything looked beautiful. The family had placed a dress code of all white instead of black as this was more of a celebration of life versus the mourning of a death.

The pastor walked up to the pulpit and began delivering the eulogy. There was not a dry eye in the church as the choir sang softly in the background. The doors of the church opened, and a woman in all-black walked inside. She walked up to Ant's casket and placed her hand on it as she dropped her head low. She bent down and kissed his casket, leaving the imprint of her red lipstick. She looked extremely out of place being the only one in black while everyone else was in all-white.

She turned around and walked over to Ant's mother and sisters. She looked into their tear filled eyes before she spoke. "So, y'all wasn't even gon' tell me my baby daddy was dead? I had to find this out in the streets? Y'all just didn't want me at the funeral so bad that you wouldn't reach out?" the woman asked.

The entire church was in awe as they looked on at the woman standing in the front of the church, yelling at the top of her lungs. The pastor had even stopped speaking, and the choir was no longer singing, allowing the women to have the conversation.

"Lashay, get out. You know you and Anthony didn't even talk. You were not invited for a reason. I didn't want to cause a scene at my son's funeral the way that you're doing now. Please just leave," June spoke.

"I'm not going anywhere. Me and my daughter have every

right to be here. Just like his other daughter and baby mama," Lashay yelled, pointing over at Shanté.

"Get the fuck out now!" Brianna's aunt yelled out, tired of Lashay's shenanigans.

"As long as this homewrecking bitch here, I'll be here too," Lashay spoke, this time looking directly at Shanté.

Brianna couldn't take it anymore. She stood to her feet and walked over to Lashay. "Look, I don't know who the fuck you are, or why you here, but my uncle didn't have no kids. So, ain't no way you his baby mama. I don't know what you want, but what you not gon' do is cause a scene at my uncle's funeral. Now, my grandmother has already asked you to leave so just leave before I drag you out."

"Your uncle? So, y'all still ain't told this baby the truth, huh? Y'all ain't shit, ain't never been shit. This ain't yo uncle, baby girl. Ant was your daddy. Not only did Ant have a daughter with me, he cheated on me with yo mama and made you. So, you have a sister."

Brianna turned and looked at her mother, and the look on her face told Brianna what the woman was saying was indeed true. Before Brianna could say a word, Shanté lunged at Lashay, landing on top of her as she fell to the floor. Shanté punched Lashay in the face repeatedly, not letting up.

Aspen and Justice quickly sprang into action, pulling Shanté off of her. "Bitch, how dare yo bitter ass come in here and start shit? This is a fuckin' funeral, you ghetto ass hood rat. And you wonder why Ant didn't fuck with you!" Shanté yelled.

"He didn't fuck with me because you kept throwing the pussy at him. It wasn't enough for you to have just one. You needed both of the brothers. You fuckin' whore. Then, on top of that, you wasn't even woman enough to tell yo own daughter who her real father was. You a trash ass bitch. That's what you are."

Brianna stormed out of the church. This was all becoming too much for her to handle. She needed some fresh air and some time to clear her head. Loke rushed out after her, grabbing her before she fell to the ground.

"My uncle is my daddy?" Brianna whispered, looking up at Loke with tears streaming down her face.

Aspen and Justice quickly followed, walking out the church, trying to find Brianna. "Bri, are you okay?" Justice asked, running over to her.

"No! How the hell can I be okay, and I don't even know who the fuck I am? How the fuck can my uncle be my father? Why would they lie to me all this time?" Brianna was crushed. She tried to come up with a reason for why they would lie to her, but she came up with nothing.

Shanté came out the church and walked up to Brianna. "Brianna, we need to talk," Shanté ordered.

"Then talk. Say what you got to say cause I'm ready to hear it."

"Can we talk in private?" she asked, looking around at Loke, Aspen, and Justice.

"Why? I wasn't told this shit in private. Hell, the whole church knows that I don't know who the fuck I am. So just say what you gotta say now."

"Brianna, I am still your mother. You will not stand here and disrespect me," Shanté shot back.

Brianna recoiled, looking over at her mother in disgust. "My mother? Girl, bye. You ain't no mother to me. Yo name is Shanté, and right now, you just some bitch that broke my heart and lied to me my whole life. Fuck you!" Brianna yelled out before walking away.

She had no words for her mother. The pain she was feeling was unexplainable. Here she was, thinking she was laying her uncle to rest, and all the while, it was her father. On top of that, someone she didn't even know was the person that told her. It was not even her own mother, the woman who was supposed to love her and protect her from pain. Loke was right behind Brianna as she got into her car and pulled off down the street. Both Justice and Aspen stood there in shock, not knowing what to say.

"I didn't mean to lie to my baby. I just didn't know what else to do," Shanté cried, looking over at Justice and Aspen. Aspen's heart went out to Shanté. Brianna was her best friend, and she loved her like a sister. At the same time, Shanté was like a mother to her. Shanté had been there for Aspen when no one else was. Shanté had taught Aspen how to drive, how to pay bills, everything she needed to turn her into the woman she was today.

Aspen walked over to Shanté, hugging her lovingly. She explained to her that Brianna would need time to process everything that had taken place, promising her that, at some point, Brianna would at least calm down enough to listen to her side of the story.

"Thank you, Aspen," Shante replied before walking back into the church.

"I CAN'T BELIEVE my own mother would lie to me like that. Then, she had the nerve to try to tell me to respect her. Man, fuck that bitch!" Brianna yelled, walking into her house, and throwing her keys on the table.

"I'm so sorry this happened to you, baby."

Loke walked over to Brianna and held her tightly. She cried into his arms, not understanding how this happened. Her doorbell rang, and she immediately knew it was Justice and Aspen. Loke walked to the door, allowing them inside.

"Bri, I'm so sorry, girl." Justice spoke sympathetically as she rushed over to hug her cousin. Aspen quickly joined in, making it a three-person hug.

"Why would she do me like that, y'all?" Brianna cried. Her soul was broken. She felt as though she didn't even know herself anymore.

"Talk to her, hear her reasoning for what she did," Aspen suggested.

"Fuck her. I don't ever want to talk to her again. I can't believe shit she say. Everything she done said this far has been a fuckin lie. She let some bitch come off the street and tell me who my father really was. Type shit is that?" Brianna continued.

"Bri, Auntie Shanté loves you. I think if you just…"

"I said fuck that bitch! Now, whose side y'all on? Coming in here, telling me I should listen to her. When I was listening to her, she wasn't doin' shit but lying," she continued.

"We on yo side, Bri. You know that. We just sayin' that if you want answers, you gonna have to talk to someone to get them," Aspen reasoned.

"I will. I'm going to talk to my daddy. I mean, my uncle or whatever the fuck he is to me," Brianna answered.

CHAPTER FIFTEEN

Brianna woke up early Saturday morning and got dressed. She was on her way to Gus Harrison Correctional Facility. She was going to visit her daddy, hoping to get answers to her questions. He'd been in prison most of Brianna's life, going in when she was only nine years old. She drove the hour-long ride in silence, with only the thoughts in her head to keep her company.

When she stepped into the prison, she felt as though she would have a panic attack. She began to feel lightheaded and broke out into a sweat. She tried to calm herself down, knowing she was there to hear the truth. Brianna was escorted into the visitation room and took a seat at the table. Several moments later, she watched her daddy walk into the room. Darius Clark stood six feet tall with smooth caramel complimented skin. His huge muscles gave him a cocky look as he walked in, owning the entire room. Even in chains, he was the shit, and he knew it. He got supreme respect behind the wall, and nobody wanted to get on his bad side. Darius smiled when he saw her, not expecting to see Brianna as his visitor.

"How's Daddy's baby girl doing? This is a pleasant surprise. I've missed you so much."

"Did you know that Uncle Ant was my biological father?" Brianna asked, cutting right to the chase. She'd been lied to long enough and was ready for the truth, even if it was the saddest thing she'd ever heard.

"Who the fuck told you that?" Darius shot back. Brianna could see the vein forming in his forehead, so she knew he was upset.

"Is it true?" Brianna replied in a no-nonsense tone.

"I am your daddy, Brianna. I was there when you came out of your mother. I cut your cord and held you for the first time. I've loved you since the day you were born. Made sure you had everything you needed. Daddy daughter dances, I was there. That alone makes me your father," Darius spoke.

"I get all that, and it's all true. But did you help create me though is what I'm asking?"

Darius dropped his head, rubbing his hands over his eyes before he responded. "No, I didn't. But just because you make a baby doesn't mean you're the father."

"Actually, that's exactly what it means. Why would y'all do that to me? Why not just tell me the truth? This some fucked up, *Jerry Springer* ass shit. Like what fuckin' trailer park did y'all come out of? Because who the fuck grows up with their daddy as they uncle and they uncle as their daddy? Did y'all not think about how bad this could fuck me up? I literally can't trust none of y'all," Brianna spat, pissed that her family had been lying to her for all these years.

"Bri, it's not that simple. I was a fucked up person at one point. So fucked up that I did some horrible things to your mother. So, when she stepped out on me with my own brother, I had no choice but to accept it. To forgive her just as she'd forgiven me so many times before. When she found out she was pregnant, we all knew it was Ant's baby. We all decided that since me and yo mama was gonna stay together that it was best if I raised you as my own. Ant wasn't ready to be a father. He had some other woman pregnant at the time, and he was already trying to get out of being a father to that child. It might seem fucked up, but me and your mother love you. So, we thought we were doing the right thing at the time."

"So, y'all was only thinking about y'all selves and what y'all wanted and not what was best for me?"

"We did what was best for you, Brianna. You had two parents that loved you and took care of you."

"Right, until you went to prison and left me and Mama. Meanwhile, my real father was still walking the streets, playing the uncle role. Looks to me like none of y'all thought about me or my feelings. I had to hear about this from someone I don't even know. None of y'all told me."

"Brianna, this was never supposed to happen. You were

never even supposed to find out," Darius spoke sympathetically.

"I wasn't supposed to find out? Are you fuckin' serious right now?!"

Brianna had heard enough. In her eyes, she was the only one hurt. Everyone had gotten what they wanted but her. Ant was able to live his life without being tied down to the responsibilities of being a father. Her mother got to keep her man, and her father got the daughter he wanted. She was the only one that had lost out on anything.

She stood from the table and began to walk off. Darius called out to her, urging her to come back and talk to him, but she couldn't. Tears streamed down her face as she thought about the horrible way her family had treated her.

She got into her car and immediately drove off, wanting to get as far away from the prison as she could. Tears still streaming down her face, she pulled over and attempted to get herself together. She'd never gone through this type of trauma before and had no idea how to cope with her feelings. So, she sat there, on the side of the road, crying uncontrollably.

After about fifteen minutes of crying, she was finally able to get herself together enough to drive home where Loke was waiting for her. He could see the pain all over her face when she walked in the door. He pulled her close, embracing her lovingly as he kissed her forehead.

"What you need me to do, baby?" Loke asked.

"Just hold me," Brianna replied.

· · ·

ASPEN SAT in the visitation room of Huron Valley, waiting for Cove to walk in. She needed to know who told Cove about them hitting licks. She was almost positive that whoever had found them out was responsible for Ant's murder, and she wanted to know who it was.

"Who told you about us?" Aspen asked as soon as Cove took her seat and the CO walked away.

"Why does that matter? I gave you the drop, so that's all you need to know."

"I'm not playing games with you, Cove. Ant is dead."

"Who the fuck is Ant?" Cove asked in genuine confusion.

"Brianna's uncle. He was the one helping us. Somebody came into his house and killed him."

"I don't know nothing about any of that," Cove stated firmly.

"I didn't think that you would. I'm just asking you who told you it was us. Whoever said it has to have some kind of connection to one of the people we hit. I'm just trying to find out who killed Ant," Aspen spoke, keeping her voice at a low whisper.

"And what you gon' do if you find out who killed him? Stop talkin' crazy, Aspen. You getting' in too deep with this shit. The game ain't to be played with, and you gettin' in over yo head."

Cove knew the game all too well. So, she knew how it

could swallow a person up whole before chewing them up and spiting them out, causing them to make horrible decisions, similar to the one Aspen was getting ready to make. The truth was nobody told Cove Aspen and her friends were hittin' licks. Cove figured it out on her own. Word spread around the prison of trap houses being hit by three men. She already knew her sister was getting to the money from talking to Shanté. They just didn't know where it was coming from. At first, Cove thought it was their boyfriends that were hittin' the licks until Aspen came to visit her, and Cove saw the look of money all in her eyes. That was the moment when she realized it was them.

"You told me you were hittin' licks, Aspen. I don't know anything about nobody bein' killed. But what I do know is y'all pissed off a lot of big niggas on the streets. So, ain't no tellin' who know y'all did that shit. You need to be careful, lil' sis."

"Wait, so nobody actually told you it was us?" Aspen asked, confused.

"You told me. It was all over yo face when you came to see me. Look, I wasn't tryna knock yo hustle. I just wanted you to know shit could get dangerous. And clearly it has," Cove responded.

Aspen was even more confused now as she looked at Cove in disbelief. "Why would you tell me someone told you it was us if it wasn't true?"

"Because I wanted you to know if I figured it out, then it was nothing stopping someone else from doing the same."

Aspen already knew that firsthand from the night Moe had come into her house. She knew she couldn't be mad at her sister because everything she was saying made sense. Aspen also knew that put them back at square one with no leads on who killed Ant. She left her visit with Cove the same way she started - knowing nothing.

Aspen walked back to her truck and placed a call to Justice as soon as she got inside. If they were going to find out who killed Ant, they would need more details. She asked Justice if she wanted to ride over to Shanté's house and have a talk with her. Aspen didn't know if Shanté knew anything that might help, but she felt it was worth a try. She also wanted to check on Shanté and see how she was holding up after everything that happened. Justice agreed, and Aspen made her way to her house.

When they got to Shanté's house, they were happy to see that her car was in the driveway. The walked up to her door, and when Aspen knocked on it, it opened. Both Justice and Aspen looked at each other in confusion, and Justice pulled her 38 from her purse. They walked inside slowly, calling out for Shanté.

Her home was in disarray with turned over furniture and things scattered everywhere. They immediately knew something was wrong as they continued searching the house for Shanté, fearing the worst.

"Bitch, what the fuck is going on?" Justice asked, tiptoeing through the house alongside Aspen.

"Something ain't right. Where the fuck is Ms. Shanté at?" Aspen replied.

After searching the entire house and not finding any trace of Shanté, they knew something had happened to her. Justice pulled her phone from her purse and called Brianna. Her heartbeat rapidly as she waited for her to answer.

"What up doe?" Brianna answered.

"Bri, um… I think you should come over here to Aunt Shanté. Me and Aspen over here and the house fucked up, and we can't find her."

"I don't give a damn 'bout her. She can clean her damn house herself. Shit's not my problem. She lost me when I found out she'd been lying to me my entire life," Brianna replied, not caring to hear about her mother.

"Nah, Bri, it's not like she got an unkempt house. I think somebody came in here and took her, Bri. The house is fucked up like it was some type of fight here. Her door was open, and her car is in the driveway."

Brianna instantly sat up in bed, not believing what she was hearing. Yes, she was livid with her mother for lying to her, but she didn't want any harm to come to her. She jumped out of bed, moving swiftly, putting on a pair of sweatpants.

"Where you going?" Loke asked as he watched Brianna put on a pair of white Nikes.

She didn't answer him; she had no time. She had to get to

her mother's house and find out what was going on. She jumped into her car, pulling off down the street, not giving a damn about the speed limits.

She arrived at her mother's house within fifteen minutes. Justice and Aspen were sitting inside Aspen's truck, which was parked in the driveway. She jumped out of her car, running up to them immediately.

"Did y'all find her?" Brianna asked.

"She's not in the house, Bri." Justice spoke sympathetically.

Brianna ran into the house, screaming out for her mother. However, she was halted at the door at the way the house looked. She knew immediately someone had come into the house, and something had happened to her mother. She looked in her mother's bedroom closet where she kept her money and other valuables, and they were all still there. *This wasn't no damn robbery,* Brianna thought to herself.

Walking back into the living room, she stood there for several seconds in confusion before walking into the kitchen. There, laying on the kitchen counter, was a piece of paper. When Brianna picked it up and began reading, she realized it was a ransom letter. It stated that they had seventy-two hours to come up with ten million dollars in cash, or Shanté would be murdered.

Brianna broke down into tears as she ran to show the letter to Aspen and Justice. "Ten million dollars? How the fuck we gon' get that shit in seventy-two fucking hours?" Justice spoke.

"Well, I got two mill at the crib," Aspen offered.

"I got about a mill at the crib and probably about 500K between the safes at my salon and store," Justice stated.

"How much you got, Bri?" Aspen questioned.

"Shit, about one and some change. We still short than a muthafucka though. How the hell we gonna get the rest of it in three days?" Brianna was at her wits end and felt as if one more thing happened, she would break.

"I'ma ask Cream for some money," Justice offered.

"No! The letter say if we involve anyone else, they will kill her," Brianna reminded.

"I'm not gonna tell him why I need it. I'm just gon' say I need some money. Calm down. Bri. I promise you we gon' do everything we can to get her back."

Brianna tried to relax, but that was easier said than done. He mother had been kidnapped, and Brianna had no idea if she was hurt or not.

"I'll ask Quan too. Don't worry, Bri. We gon' get her back," Aspen reassured.

Brianna tried to think positive, but it was hard seeing how short they were on the money. Brianna knew that she wouldn't rest until her mother was back home safely. So, she vowed to do whatever she had to do to make that happen.

Justice rushed into the house, calling out for Cream as soon as she opened the door. He was sitting in the living room with a man she'd never seen before. "Hey, baby, this is my cousin, Joc. He's visiting from out of state for a few days, and he stopped by, so we can chop it up," Cream informed.

Justice smiled and greeted Joc before letting Cream know that she needed to speak with him. He followed Justice to their bedroom.

"What's up, baby?" Cream asked, taking a seat on the bed.

"Cream, I need some cash," Justice spoke, cutting right to the chase.

Cream pulled a wad of money from his pants pocket and started counting out one-hundred-dollar bills. "You know I got you. How much you need, baby?"

"I need more than you got in your pocket."

"What's going on, Justice?"

"I got into a little problem down at my store. I need about three million."

"Three million dollars? Justice, what kind of three-million-dollar problems you having?" Cream asked.

Justice knew she couldn't tell Cream the truth, and she didn't want to involve him in her shit. However, she needed the money. There was no way she could allow those people to kill her aunt. When Justice didn't respond quickly enough, Cream spoke again.

"I know I can't get you three, but I can write you a check for a mill and a half."

"I need it in cash," Justice responded. She knew if he wrote a check, it would take several days to clear and even longer for her to withdraw that amount of money out the bank. They didn't have that type of time. They only had three days to come up with ten million dollars, so every minute counted.

"Damn, Jay, you driving a hard bargain. I'ma see what I can do. I'll let you know tomorrow."

"Thank you, baby," Justice replied, kissing Cream on the lips.

"You can thank me later when Joc leaves."

BRIANNA RUSHED home to gather the money she had. Even with all three of them putting their money together, they were still about five million short. It was no doubt that her and her girls were hustlers. However, they'd never had to come up with that much money in such a limited amount of time.

She racked her mind, trying to come up with ways to get the money, but she came up with nothing. She knew her girls said they would ask their men, but she couldn't count on that. This was her mother, so it was her responsibility to assure she was okay.

She thought about hitting licks as they'd always done however quickly changed her mind. *That ain't gonna get us the money that fast, and Ant not here no more to buy the keys.* She thought about taking a bank but didn't know if she could get away with it. She definitely didn't want to get caught and end up in jail before she could get her mother back. Her thoughts were all over the place, and the bottom line was she didn't know what she was going to do.

Brianna walked inside her home, only to find that Loke wasn't there. When she called him to find out where he was, he let her know he was out handling business. He told her he would be home later that night, and they ended the call.

"Shit, I can't even ask him til later. I got to figure something out til then," Brianna spoke aloud.

She began to feel sweaty, and before she knew it, she was running to the bathroom to throw up. Her nerves were getting the best of her. She knew she wouldn't be able to calm down until her mother was home. Brianna brushed her teeth before she started gathering her money. She heard her doorbell ring, and she went to answer the door.

"Okay, Quan gave me a million, so I got three here. And don't worry, bitch. I didn't tell him why I needed it," Aspen announced, placing her duffle bag down on Brianna's kitchen table. "Justice here yet?" she continued.

Before Brianna could answer, her doorbell rang again. They both knew it was Justice, and Brianna opened the door and let her in.

"Okay, it's just under a mill and a half in this duffle bag. I asked Cream, and he said he could probably get me a million and a half by tomorrow. Did you ask Loke?" Justice spoke.

"He hasn't been home. I'm gonna ask him when he gets here tonight. But we still short. What if Cream or Loke don't have the money? How the fuck we gonna come up with five million in less than three days?"

"Calm down, Bri. We gonna think of something. We just gotta put our heads together. We gettin' Auntie Shanté back. That's on everything I love." Justice assured. "We can hit some more dope spots," she suggested.

"And do what? Ant is dead. We don't have nobody to sell the keys to," Brianna replied.

"What if we don't take the keys, just the money? If we hit enough of them, we might get the money we need," Aspen agreed.

Brianna thought for a moment. It was worth a try. She would rather be getting any amount of money instead of sitting on her ass, thinking about needing money. So, with that, she agreed. They planned to hit every single trap house they knew about that next day.

CHAPTER SIXTEEN

*S*hanté sat in a smelly, unfinished basement, chained to a chair. She looked around, trying to see if anything or anybody was down there with her, but she was alone. There was nothing but the chair she sat in and a small table across from her in the entire basement. There was only one dim light in the far corner of the room which hung from the ceiling. It only lit that one corner, and the rest of the basement was dark. It was damp down there, and Shanté was cold from the chill that was in the air. Her mouth was dry, and she felt dehydrated as she tried to lick her lips to moisten them. Shanté attempted to free herself from the chains, shaking and rattling them, trying to break free. However, nothing she did worked.

Shanté had no idea who had brought her there or what they wanted with her. She just knew she had to get away. She had fucked up by letting them get her. She knew that once they got you, they had you. So, the odds were already against her.

Shanté was just about to run herself a bubble bath when two masked men burst into her home. She tried to fight back as best she could, but she was no match for the two strong men. She ran in circles around her house, throwing everything she came in contact with at the men, in an effort to get away. One of them hit her in the face so hard that she was knocked out cold. When she'd finally woken up, she was chained to a chair in a dark basement. She was scared, to say the least, and didn't see a way out of her situation at the moment.

She wasn't even sure if anyone knew she was even missing yet. Shanté knew the longer she was there, the less likely it was that anyone would find her. She didn't know who the men were or what they wanted. She hadn't even seen them since she'd regained consciousness, and she was overwhelmed with fear as the realization that she was kidnapped came to the light.

"Hello!" Shanté called out several times, hoping someone would come to her. She wanted to know what they wanted with her, so maybe then, she would be able to figure out an escape or at least get them what they wanted, so they would let her go. She had no clue what was going on and just wanted someone to talk to her.

She prayed she could find a way to get away unharmed. *I can't die like this. I haven't even told my daughter I was sorry for hurting her. I can't die with my daughter hating me. She has to know that I love her and that I'm sorry for lying to her. I got to get the fuck outta here.* Shanté had never been in this situation before. She wasn't in the street life. She didn't have enemies or owe anyone any money. So, she couldn't understand why someone would do this to her of all people. *This has to be some kind of mistake,* she thought as tears continued to fall from her eyes.

Shanté continued to call out to whoever was inside the house. She hoped, at the very least, that they would get tired of hearing her screaming and come down to check on her. After what seemed like hours of screaming at the top of her lungs and nobody coming down to her, Shanté finally stopped. Her mouth was beyond dry, and she'd became the one tired of hearing herself scream. She felt defeated as she realized all she could do was wait it out.

Aspen made her way home, exhausted from the day's events. She knew she was going to have a very long day tomorrow, and all she wanted to do was relax. She pulled into her drive-way, getting out her G-wagon and walking into her house. She heard the soft sounds of H.E.R. singing about loving her man in every kinda way, and she smiled. She looked down at her feet and saw a path of lit candles for her to walk through. She smiled as Quan greeted her at the door with a single long stemmed red rose.

"What's all this?" Aspen asked, inhaling the sweet scent of the flower.

"It's our date night, pretty lady. And I have dinner prepared for us," Quan replied. He took Aspen by the hand and led her through the candlelit path and into the dining room. There was seafood pasta in a creamy alfredo sauce, Caesar salad, and warm bread plated on a candlelit table.

"Would you like me to pour you a glass of wine?" Quan asked.

Aspen nodded her head yes, and Quan poured them both a glass. Then, they made a toast to their beautiful future with lots of love and happiness. They sat and ate a delicious dinner together, enjoying each other's company. They were both truly happy with one another and were both falling deeper and deeper in love by the day. Aspen couldn't have asked for a better man to come into her life. After the heartbreak she'd experienced, she was happy to finally have a man she knew truly loved her.

When they were done eating, Quan led Aspen to the bathroom where he ran her a bubble bath. There were rose petals and candles lit all around the bathroom, and Aspen couldn't help but to feel special. Aspen undressed and stepped down into the bathtub, letting the warm water and bubbles cover her body. Quan gently washed every part of Aspen's body for her, and she enjoyed every minute of it. This was exactly what she needed after the day she'd had.

Quan helped her out the tub and wrapped a towel around

her before carrying her to their bed. He laid her down and gently spread her legs. "I wanna make you feel good, baby," he whispered, placing his face between her thighs. Quan allowed his tongue to find her love button, and she moaned softly. He feasted on her like she was his last meal, savoring every lick until she overflowed.

Quan climbed on top of Aspen, kissing her lips gently. His manhood was thick and hard as he pushed it inside her wetness, filling her up with his thickness. She moaned louder, clutching his back tightly as he pumped in and out of her. They made love all night until they both fell asleep in each other's arms, feeling more in love than ever before.

That next morning, Aspen woke up early, before Quan got out of bed, and got dressed. She packed her disguise inside her duffle bag and walked out the house, headed to Brianna's. She knew they had a lot of ground to cover today, and they all wanted to make sure they got an early start. Justice hadn't gotten the money from Cream yet, but he promised her he would get it later on that day. Loke had also told Brianna that he would try to get as much as possible by the end of the day. They walked out the house and made their way to their first hit.

SHANTÉ SAT IN THE CHAIR, screaming for someone to come to her yet again. Her mouth was dry, and her lips were now cracking. She just needed some water and maybe some food.

She was beginning to feel weak, and her stomach growled loudly. She had no idea how long she'd been down there because all of the windows in the basement were covered with cardboard. Finally, after what seemed like hours of her screaming, she heard a door open and footsteps walking down the stairs. She was both relieved and nervous as the person approached.

She saw a man walk over to her. He was tall and muscular but had a mask covering his face. So, she had no idea who it was. The man placed a bottled water and a paper plate with a bologna sandwich on a small table he placed in front of her. He unchained one of her hands so that she would be able to eat.

"Why am I here?" Shanté asked the man as she looked down at the plain sandwich, turning her nose up to it. She was indeed hungry but didn't know if she could trust the food he'd given her. When he didn't answer her, she spoke again. "What do you want with me?"

The man didn't speak. Instead, he just looked down at Shanté. There was no need for him to say anything. He'd already stated what he wanted, and he was sure someone was working on getting it. Shanté attempted to study the man's eyes in an effort to figure out who he was, but it was to no avail. She didn't recognize the man at all, and with a mask covering his face, she wouldn't be able to give a description.

"Can you please just answer my questions? I just want to know why I'm here! How can I get you what you want if you won't even tell me what that is?" Shanté yelled. She was becoming frustrated at the man for not talking. She needed to know why she'd been kidnapped so that maybe she could give them what they wanted, and she could get away.

The man turned around and walked away, heading back up the stairs, without saying a word. Shanté took the bottle of water, opening the top and smelling it to assure it was actually water. When she didn't smell anything, she put the bottle to her lips and took a small sip. Realizing it was indeed water, she gulped it down, giving her body much needed hydration. She wanted to eat the sandwich but decided against it, leaving it sitting on the table. She needed to use the bathroom but didn't think the man would come back down the stairs. So, instead of calling out to him, she sat there, trying to hold in her urine.

She heard the door open and could hear voices but couldn't make out what they were saying. She was able to hear that it was at least one woman that was talking, but she couldn't tell how many men there were. She tried to listen in, but their voices were so low that she couldn't make out anything. She thought that someone was coming back down to her; however, when she heard the door close and didn't hear any footsteps, she knew no one was coming.

Tears began to fill her eyes and run down her face. She just wanted to go home. She wanted to see her daughter again. She wanted to hug her and tell her how sorry she was for the lies she told. She promised God that if she made it out alive, she would fix her relationship with her daughter and never lie again.

ASPEN DROVE off from their fifth hit of the day. They had two duffle bags filled with money but didn't know the total. They made their way to the freeway, heading to Inkster. There were two spots out there they would hit before going back to Brianna's house to count the money they had so far. They turned down Avondale, parking their car in front of the house. They all got out, walking up onto the porch, and Justice knocked. Once the door was opened, they burst through, guns in hand.

They ordered the man to put all the money in the bag while they held him at gunpoint. The man hurriedly gathered up all the money and placed it into the duffle bag. When they had what they'd come for, they walked out the door and headed to their car.

When they got to Brianna's house, they emptied the money out of the duffle bags onto her kitchen table. The three of them got to work, counting all the money by hand. When they were done, they had eight hundred and fifty thousand dollars. Brianna couldn't do anything but drop her head.

"We never gon' come up with enough money hittin these fuckin' licks. We gotta have the money in two days." Brianna spoke in defeat.

Both Justice and Aspen wanted to think positive. However, they were starting to think they wouldn't be able to come up with the money that way. The all sat in silence as they tried to think of ways to come up with the money.

"Let's just go hit some more licks. We can't just sit here and let the time pass us by," Justice suggested.

They all agreed, walking out of Brianna's house. Brianna got into the driver's seat and pulled off. They decided they would go hit Fabo's spot. Although they'd robbed him once before, that was through Moe. They had never hit him directly, and they had never hit his trap house. They hoped the hit would deem to be lucrative because they were running out of options.

The sun was beginning to set, making the sky pink in color. They made their way down Southfield freeway and got off on Six Mile. They were sitting there, waiting for the light to turn green, when a black car pulled up alongside them. Everything seemed to happen so fast as the windows of the car rolled down and the passengers aimed their guns at their car. Aspen yelled out "Gun!" before ducking down in her seat, covering her head with her arms. Before Brianna could pull off, bullets started raining down on them, hitting their car and everything else that surrounded it. Every second felt like an hour as their car was riddled with bullets. The gunshots stopped, and the car skirted off, leaving behind nothing but shell casings and broken glass.

"Oh, my God. Are y'all okay? Who the fuck was that? Did you see who it was?" Aspen asked, yelling out frantically. She shook in fear, not knowing what to do.

"Yeah, I'm good. Justice, you good?" Brianna questioned, brushing the broken glass from her lap. "I don't know who the hell that was. Everything happened so fast," she continued.

When Justice didn't answer, Brianna spoke again, turning around to assure that Justice had heard her. That was when she saw Justice laying in the backseat, covered in blood and broken glass.

"Justice!" Brianna screamed, quickly climbing to the backseat to check on her cousin.

Justice wasn't moving, and there was so much blood that Brianna couldn't tell where it was coming from. She screamed for Aspen to drive them to a hospital as fast as she could as she attempted to clean the glass off Justice's body. Aspen, shaking frantically, got into the driver's seat, and pulled off down Six Mile, heading to the hospital. She didn't thing about anything but the safety of her friend as she did seventy miles per hour down Outer Drive, not stopping at a single traffic light.

CHAPTER SEVENTEEN

They arrived at the hospital just a few moments later, and Brianna rushed in to get help. She was frantic, and Justice's blood was all over her as she screamed out that she needed a doctor. Brianna was hysterical as several nurses ran over to her, thinking she was the one hurt.

"Come with me, ma'am, and tell me what happened. Where are you bleeding from, and how did you get hurt?" one of the nurses asked.

"It's not me. It's my cousin. She's out in the car. She's been shot," Brianna revealed. One of the nurses told another nurse to page a doctor before running outside. Another nurse grabbed a gurney and began wheeling it out toward the car while a doctor ran from behind two double doors and outside to the car.

Aspen jumped out as she watched the doctor and nurses come to Justice's side. There was so much blood in the backseat, and all she could do was pray that Justice wasn't dead. *Oh, my God, this is all our fault, and it's all connected. Ant's murder, Ms. Shanté's kidnapping, and our ambush. Somebody is gunnin' for us,* Aspen realized.

Justice was rushed into the hospital and immediately went into surgery. "You ladies can sit in the waiting room. Because this was a shooting, we will have to contact the authorities. They will probably need a statement from the two of you since the two of you brought her in," a nurse informed before walking away.

"Oh, my God, I hope she's going to be okay. She can't die, Aspen," Brianna cried.

Aspen wanted to break down, but she knew she would have to be the strong one. Brianna was in shambles and couldn't take any more bad news.

"I hope so too. We gotta call her mama and Cream." Aspen spoke, pulling her phone from her purse.

She dialed them both, letting them know the hospital she was in, before walking into the waiting room. She wished that this was all a bad dream and that someone would be waking her up soon. But every time she pinched herself, she knew it was real. *God, please let her be okay,* Aspen prayed silently.

"Bitch, what are we gon' tell the police when they get here?" Brianna asked.

"Shit, we gon' tell them what happened. We was stopped at a red light when a car pulled up and started shooting at us. That's exactly what happen," Aspen replied.

"You don't think they gon' ask us any other questions? Like where we were going?"

"Who cares where we were going? Justice is the victim, and we witnessed her shooting. I doubt they gonna treat us like anything other than that. We don't have to tell them no extra shit, Bri," Aspen informed.

Brianna nodded her head and sat back in her seat, seemingly relaxing. She knew Aspen was right. They were just sitting at a red light when everything happened. So, whatever they were doing before that shouldn't matter.

"Bitch, what about the guns? They still in the car under the seat," Brianna recalled, sitting up in her chair just a few seconds later.

Aspen had forgotten all about the guns the moment they had realized Justice had been shot. Her only focus had been making sure she got Justice to the hospital. "I'm gonna go to the car and get them. If the police get here before I get back, just tell them I went to the bathroom or something," Aspen replied.

Aspen quickly got up and walked out the hospital. She had no clue what she would do with the guns. All she knew was she had to get them out of the car before the police searched it. There would be no way they would be able to explain the guns to the police if they were found. Not only were the guns not registered, but they had bodies on them — bodies of men the girls had taken out themselves during a lick they'd hit. That was a mandatory two years behind bars that Aspen didn't have to give to the prison system.

Aspen all but ran to the car, removing the guns from under the seat, quickly wiping their fingerprints from them, and putting them inside her purse. She stood there, thinking for several seconds about where to put the guns. She had to find a place to put them where the police would not find them. She knew she couldn't bring them into the hospital, knowing the metal detector would go off the moment she walked inside. *God, please show me a way out of this,* Aspen silently prayed. Just like that, as if God was showing her a way out, Aspen looked down and saw Justice's purse.

"Thank you, God." Aspen spoke aloud before grabbing Justice's purse and walking off.

Justice had started the nasty habit of smoking cigarettes. Although Aspen hated them, they would definitely come in handy at the moment. The hospital was a no smoking zone, so it wouldn't look suspicious for Aspen to walk off the property for a cigarette. If the police looked at the cameras and saw her leave, she would just say she went to smoke.

She pulled one of the Newport's and a lighter from Justice's purse, walking all the way onto the main street before she lit it. She walked up the street, seemingly smoking a cigarette, when in all actuality, she was trying to spot every camera Sinai-Grace hospital had. Before she disposed of the guns in one of the trash cans on the street, she wanted to assure she wouldn't be caught on any of the cameras. She walked to the end of the street, making sure she didn't see any cameras, before placing all three guns into a trash can next to a D-dot bus stop. Aspen then went back to the waiting room, taking her seat next to Brianna.

"Brianna, Aspen, what happened to my baby?" Justice's mother asked, tears falling from her face.

Aspen's heart instantly broke for her as their eyes collided. She didn't want to tell her how it was their own fault that Justice had been shot. How could she tell Justice's mother that she was committing robberies with her and Brianna, and that was why she was shot? So, she decided to tell her the same story she was going to tell the police. She technically wasn't lying because that was exactly how it happened. She was just leaving some parts out. Even though she didn't know who, she knew why it happened.

"Who would do something like that? Everyone in the city knows my baby, always shopping at her store or getting their hair done at her salon. People show her love wherever she goes. I've seen it myself. I can't believe someone would do this," Tonya cried. Her worst fear was to bury one of her children. Children were supposed to bury their parents, not the other way around. If Justice didn't make it, Tonya knew it would be the end of her as well.

"How long has she been in surgery?" Cream asked,

walking into the waiting room. He was on his way to get the money Justice had asked him for when he got the call from Aspen about Justice being shot. He came right to the hospital, not caring about anything else but getting to Justice.

"Not long, maybe twenty minutes," Brianna responded. She feared for her cousin's life and hadn't stopped crying since Justice had been shot. Justice was her favorite cousin and had been more like a sister to her than anything. There was no way Brianna could imagine her life without her. She prayed that God would send a miracle down to Earth and save her life.

A few moments later, two officers entered the waiting room to take Aspen and Brianna's statements. Aspen did the talking while Brianna was too hysterical to say anything. The officers wrote down everything she said before asking for the keys to the car they were driving. Aspen handed them over, and the officers walked out of the room.

"I need to call Loke. I need him here with me. I can't fuckin' handle this shit," Brianna announced, taking her phone from her purse. She dialed his number, and his phone went straight to voicemail. She shot him a text before placing her phone back into her purse.

"I need you to tell me exactly what happened and don't leave shit out," Cream ordered, pulling Aspen to the side.

Aspen could see the look of both fear and anger on Cream's face as she replied. "I told y'all. We were sitting at a red light when a car drove up and just started shooting."

"Did y'all see who was in the car?"

"No," she answered.

"What kind of car was it?"

"I don't know what kind it was, but it was a dark color. Black, maybe blue," Aspen replied.

"Did you talk to Quan?" he asked.

"Not since it happened. I've been so concerned about Justice that I haven't even called him and told him what happened."

"I'm gon' kill the muthafuckas that did this shit. They not gon' live after this, and that's my fuckin' word," Cream stated.

SHANTÉ'S BLADDER was so full that it hurt. She called out for someone to come down and take her to the bathroom, but nobody answered. Tears of frustration ran down her face because she already knew what she would have to do. She closed her eyes and relieved herself, allowing the urine to run down her legs.

"This is some bullshit," she spoke out loud.

No one had been down in the basement to check on her since she'd been brought the bologna sandwich, and she feared no one would. Her mouth was dry because she'd only had one bottle of water since she'd been down there. She knew she needed water and was scared that she would die from dehydration before anyone came to save her. Hunger pains ran through her stomach, and she looked at the sand-wich, contemplating whether she should eat it or not.

She was so hungry that she didn't even care how long it had been sitting on the table. She picked up the sandwich with her free hand and bit it. The bread was hard and stale from sitting out, but she ate it anyway. A few moments later, the door opened, and the same man walked back down the stairs.

"Bitch, you stink. Yo ass needs a fuckin' shower," he shot. "How the fuck do you smell that bad? Females ain't supposed to smell like that," he continued, turning up his nose in disgust as he looked down at Shanté.

"Then let me shower. If you gon' keep me down here, the least you can do is allow me to stay clean," she replied.

He set two bottles of water and a pack of Pop-Tarts onto the table in front of her before turning around and walking away. Shanté wanted to cry as she watched the man walk back up the stairs. *Damn, he won't even allow me to shower? What kind of uncivilized bullshit is this?* she thought to herself. He returned several moments later with a bucket of water, a towel, and a bar of soap. Shanté looked at him in confusion as he set the bucket down next to her.

"What am I supposed to do with that? I can't wash myself being chained to this damn chair. I at least need to stand up," she said, looking down at the bucket.

"Bitch, if you wanna be clean, you gon' wash yoself and figure out how you gon' do it. It ain't up to me. You the one funky as fuck."

"How the fuck am I supposed to do that? You not making any sense." She spoke, looking down at the chains.

"Figure the shit out." He spoke before walking back up the stairs.

Shante looked down at the bucket, trying to figure out how she was going to wash herself while being chained to the chair. She wanted a shower. She needed to lather her entire body up and allow hot water to rinse it off. She wanted to cry as she dropped her head low in defeat. Seconds later, she lifted her head as if a light bulb had gone off. She knew exactly what she was going to do. Using her one free hand, she pulled the bucket in front of her and attempted to pull the metal handle off. After several attempts, she was finally able to break it off the bucket.

"Yes!" she said out loud.

Shanté placed the end of the handle into the lock on the chains. She jiggled it around in an effort to pick the lock. She couldn't stay down in that basement any longer and was going to do all she could in order to escape. It took her several tries, and she became frustrated after the tenth attempt.

"Come on, Shanté. You got this shit, bitch. It's now or never. You won't get another chance," she coached.

Finally, after a few more tries, she heard the lock click, and it opened. She quickly unraveled the chains, allowing them to fall to the floor. She stood from the chair, and her hips hurt, being weak from her sitting for a long amount of time. She looked around the basement for a weapon, something she could use to protect herself. She knew she would have to go upstairs if she was going to get out. However, she didn't know what was waiting for her up there and wanted to be prepared for whatever would come her way.

When she didn't see anything, she decided to make her own. Shanté was from the hood, so she knew exactly what to do. She squatted down to the floor and began scraping the end of the handle on the cement floor, trying to sharpen it. After several minutes, the end was finally sharp enough. Shanté began cautiously walking up the stairs, not wanting to make any noise and alert anyone that she was getting away. When she got to the top of the stairs, she placed her ear to the door. She listened for several seconds, trying to see if she could hear anything. Her heartbeat fast in her chest as nervousness set in. She knew she probably wouldn't get another chance to get away, so she had to make this one chance count.

Shanté slowly turned the doorknob, and it was unlocked. Thankful that she was one step closer to her freedom, she opened the door and was now standing in the kitchen of the house. Nothing about it looked familiar, and she knew she'd never been there before. As much as she wanted to know who'd taken her, she wanted to get away from them even more. Stepping farther into the kitchen, she noticed a back door. She ran up to it and attempted to open it, only to find that it had been locked by a deadbolt, and she knew she would need a key to open it. She knew she had no time to stand there and fidget with the lock, so she walked away, trying to find another way out.

She walked through the living room of the house and up to the front door. Opening the door, she felt the warm sun beaming down on her face, and she smiled. It felt good to feel the sun and to see the light of day again. She'd done it. She'd found her way out. Shanté wanted to cry knowing she was about to get away. She lifted her foot to step out onto the porch. However, before she could, Shanté was yanked back into the house with such force that it startled her.

"Oh, you a slick ass bitch, huh? How the fuck you even get out them chains? Thought you was getting away, huh? Well, it ain't none of that," the man yelled, pulling Shanté back inside and closing the door behind him.

Shanté felt both defeated and hopeless. She'd thought she was about to get away, only to be caught in the act. She'd come so far just for her hope of getting away from her kidnappers to be ripped away. She laid there on the living room floor, tears streaming down her face. She could hear someone walking into the room.

"You ain't too tough now, huh?" Lashay asked, looking down at Shanté.

"What the fuck? Lashay, you kidnapped me? Bitch, are you crazy?" Shanté asked. "Why the fuck would you do this? What the fuck do you even want?" she continued.

She was no longer in fear as anger came over her. She

wanted to kill Lashay and vowed to herself that she would do just that. She would have never suspected that Lashay would have anything to do with this. Ant's funeral was the first time in years that Shanté had even seen Lashay, and she didn't understand what the beef was. She sat down in a dark ass basement, fearing for her life, all for nothing. Now, as she looked up at Lashay, all she wanted to do was beat the hell out of her. Shanté stood to her feet, walking up closer to Lashay, only to be knocked back down from behind.

THE DOCTOR WALKED into the waiting room several hours later and walked up to them. "Are you all family of Justice Lewis?" she asked.

"Yes, I am her mother."

"Hello, Ms. Lewis, I am Doctor Michaels, and I was the head surgeon in your daughter's surgery. She is out of surgery now; however, she will need another. We are looking to perform that tomorrow. She suffered from two bullet wounds to her torso, one of which punctured her lung, and the other punctured her kidney. We are not able to repair her lung, but we were able to take the bullet out. With her kidney being ruptured, she will need a transplant, and it will have to be no later than tomorrow if we want to…." The doctor took a long pause, hating to say these words to the families of her patients.

"If you want to what?" Tonya asked, already knowing

what the doctor was saying. However, she needed to hear the words come out of her mouth.

"If we want to keep her alive. We are able to put her on a transplant list; however, it would be a longer wait. If anyone is willing to be tested to see if they are a match and are willing to donate one of their kidneys, that would be faster."

"Test me. Let's go," Cream called out, walking up to the doctor. He would do anything for Justice, so this was no different. Justice was the love of his life, and there was no way he could lose her.

"Yeah, test me too. My baby has to make it." Tonya spoke.

"We will need insurance cards for everyone that is being tested, as well as Ms. Lewis' card," Doctor Michaels stated.

Tonya dropped her head low, knowing that neither her nor Justice had any type of insurance.

"What's the cost of the surgery without insurance?" Cream asked.

"I'm not sure. I can have someone come and speak with you all that will know that information. I will tell you this. Without a successful transplant, she will not make it."

With those words, Tonya, Brianna, and Aspen all broke out into tears. They knew they had to do something quickly if Justice was going to have a chance at life. They watched as the doctor walked out the room.

"I need some air." Brianna spoke before storming out the room. Everything was becoming too much for her, and she couldn't take anymore.

Aspen walked out after her friend, wanting to comfort her even though she was just as hurt.

"Bri, wait up," she called out.

Brianna turned around, face full of tears. "This is too much. We don't even have the money to get my mama back, and now, we have to also come up with money for Justice's surgery? How the fuck are we gonna make sure they both stay alive?" she cried.

"We got this. We just gon' do what we gotta do. We gon' save them both if that's the last thing I'ma do. Once we find out how much the surgery will be, we'll go from there," Aspen spoke.

Brianna's phone rang, and she looked at it, hoping it was Loke. She needed him at this moment as she tried to keep her sanity. She saw it was a number she didn't know but decided to answer it anyway.

"I hope you gettin' my fuckin' money," a male voice spoke into the phone. Brianna had never heard the voice before and had no clue who it was.

"Where is my mama?" she asked.

"She's safe for now, but she won't be if you don't get me my money. I'll be calling you tomorrow with a time and location. If you don't have my shit, I will have no problem killing your mother, along with everyone else you love," the man stated smugly before ending the call.

"That was them? What they say?" Aspen asked.

"The gon' kill her if we don't come up with the money. Aspen, what the fuck are we gon' do? Between my mama and Justice, we out of hella money that we don't have."

Aspen knew all this was their own fault, and she wished she could rewind time and do things differently. She wished they would have never came up with a plan to get revenge on Moe because everything started there. She would have never allowed her or her friends to make a career of hitting licks. They had involved people that didn't have anything to do with what they were doing, and those were the people that ended up hurt. Aspen felt responsible for everything that transpired, and she wished that she had the solution to fix it.

"We just got to keep putting our heads together. I'm sure we will come up with something. Even if we gotta go up in that muthafucka and get her ourselves."

Brianna looked up at Aspen as if a light bulb had gone off. "That don't sound like a bad idea. If we go get her, we can use the money we got for Justice's surgery," Brianna spoke.

Just like that, it was like weight had been lifted off Brianna's shoulders as they had finally come up with a plan. They walked back into the hospital, feeling more at ease about the situation. When they got back up to Justice's floor, they heard the alarm going off, and the computerized voice chanting "code red." They ran to the waiting room where they saw Tonya standing outside the door, screaming out in sheer agony.

"My baby, please save my baby!" She yelled before falling to the floor, feeling helpless.

To be continued...

Did you enjoy the read?
Let us know how much by leaving us a review on Amazon and Goodreads.

OTHER BOOKS BY

<u>URBAN AINT DEAD</u>

Tales 4rm Da Dale

The Hottest Summer Ever

Hittin' Licks For The Holidays: Atlanta

Wet Dreams On Lockdown: The Nurse

By **Elijah R. Freeman**

Despite The Odds

By **Juhnell Morgan**

Good Girl Gone Rogue

By **Manny Black**

Hittaz

Hittaz 2

Hittaz 3

Hittaz 4

Coldhearted

By **Lou Garden Price, Sr.**

Charge It To The Game

Charge It To The Game 2

A Summer To Remember With My Hitta

Snatched Up By A Hitta

Santa Sent Me A Real One For Christmas

Wet Dreams on Lockdown: The Unit Manager

Thug Me The Right Way 2

By **Nai**

A Setup For Revenge

Wet Dreams On Lockdown: The Librarian

By **Ashley Williams**

Ridin' For You

Trickin' on a Heaux for Christmas: A BBW Love Story

Homie Hoppin' For The Holidays

Wet Dreams on Lockdown: The Female C.O

By **Telia Teanna**

The State's Witness

The State's Witness 2

The State's Witness 3

By **Kyiris Ashley**

Stuck In The Trenches

Stuck In The Trenches 2

By **Huff Tha Great**

The Swipe

By **Toōla**

Melted the Heart of a Menace

Wet Dreams On Lockdown: Lieutenant Grace

By P. Wise

Merry Trapmas: Ice & Frost

By **Mia Sky**

Thug Me The Right Way

By **DiamondATL & Nai**

Wet Dreams on Lockdown: The Male C.O

By **Tamyra Griffin**

Wet Dreams On Lockdown: The Counselor

By **Paris Iman**

Wet Dreams On Lockdown: The Warden

By **Shawnice**

Wet Dreams On Lockdown: The Captain

By **TN Jones**

BOOKS BY

URBAN AINT DEAD's C.E.O

<u>Elijah R. Freeman</u>

Triggadale

Triggadale 2

Triggadale 3

Tales 4rm Da Dale

The Hottest Summer Ever

Murda Was The Case

Murda Was The Case 2

Murda Was The Case 3

Hittin' Licks For The Holidays: Atlanta

Wet Dreams On Lockdown: The Nurse

STAY CONNECTED

Follow
Elijah R. Freeman
On Social Media
FB: Elijah R. Freeman
IG: @the_future_of_urban_fiction